Through Minty Meadows

The emptying train…
Puffs out of Egloskerry to Tresmeer
Through minty meadows…

John Betjeman

For my dear mother, Phyl Northey.
Also in memory of her family, the Gynns,
who lived at Killicoff in the early part of the 20th century.

ISBN 978-0–9563990–9–0

Printed by R Booth Ltd, Penryn Cornwall

Chapter 1.

The road from Launceston to Egloskerry flattened out after the steep, tortuous climb up the hill to St. Stephen's with its cluster of slate-roofed cottages. The pony and trap made its way steadily now past the forested lane to the right, which wound around the darkness of evergreen trees. The light was failing and the driver of the small trap was bent over his reins, urging the tired pony on, making him pick up his hooves and quicken his pace towards home.

Below the ribbon of road could be seen farm buildings almost hidden down an overgrown lane and in the fading distance was the tall tower of the village church, dedicated to Stephen the Martyr. Across the valley, the market town of Launceston with its distinctive Norman castle and its narrow winding streets, was obscured now with the gathering darkness.

Birds and small animals could be heard rustling in the hedges and trees as the pony clip-clopped along the narrow road towards Egloskerry. The man started nervously and pulled his coat collar up when an owl screeched nearby from a tall tree. The trap passed the turning to the hamlet of Langore quickly for the pony seemed to pick up speed, perhaps sensing that home and a feed of oats would be waiting at the end of the four-mile journey from Launceston.

A farmhouse on the left was silhouetted against a crescent moon, its tall chimneys clear to be seen. Oil lamps lit up two downstairs windows, square blocks of yellow light in the gloom. Over the stables a young lad looked out of a window with a flickering candle in his hand, on hearing the sharp metallic hooves trotting along the roadway. But his interest lapsed when the trap bowled along past.

The trap-driver clicked his teeth at the pony and lightly touched him with the reins. A spurt of energy ensued as the animal commenced the long downhill slope through the trees towards Little Athill.

A closer look at the man driving the trap revealed him to be quite youthful in appearance, ruddy-faced beneath his hat which was pulled well down over his eyes, which were dark and rather fine. His whole aspect seemed to be one of nervousness, his body held taut as a frightened wild animal.

The pony and trap dipped down to the long farm buildings at Little Athill which were clothed in darkness. Somewhere in the barn a cow helved mournfully, as if her calf had been recently taken away from her. Again there was the screech of an owl, which unseated the man momentarily so that he dropped the reins and the pony lurched in panic.

Out of the darkness four figures appeared from behind the barn, lit briefly by the moon. One grabbed the reins and pulled the frightened, floundering pony to a standstill. Two others wrenched the man from the wooden trap and dragged him, kicking, into the nearby ditch. The fourth man, as thin as a weasel in appearance, looked nervously around as he watched the vicious beating.

It did not last long. The men rummaged through the man's clothing, picking over him like vultures. They soon found the man's leather pouch with its precious coins from a day at the market and ran off into the shadows.

'We'll have a few drinks in the Simcoe Arms tomorrow,' crowed the weasel-faced man in an unknown accent. The men soon scarpered across the fields away from the Chapel, ominous Red Down looming above them in the moonlit distance.

The young man was left in the ditch, battered and bleeding. The moon's silvery light gently caressed his swollen, unrecognizable features as he slept what seemed to be the sleep of the dead.

Chapter 2.

Mary Jane Jenkin opened the back door of the farmhouse at Badharlick, letting gleams of early sunlight filter into the back scullery. She shivered and pulled her woollen shawl tightly around her and tied it behind her waist. The morning was grey and chilly for it was still early, but her work as milkmaid for the house cows required an early start and she knew no different. The farmhouse seemed to lie sleeping, but she knew that Sarah would soon be raking over the ashes and lighting the fire in its huge granite fireplace.

As she crossed the farmyard, a cockerel crowed loudly from his perch on the gate. Mary Jane clanked her tin buckets at him to shoo him away, but he persisted in preening his bright feathers and in making himself heard far across the misty valley.

Mary Jane washed the buckets thoroughly at the pump with its granite trough, shivering as the cold sparkling water splashed over her hands and her apron of coarse sacking. Water ran out of the trough into the muck of the yard and her work-boots squelched as she lifted her feet. She started to make her way through the filth to the barn, where the three house cows were still lying, chewing the cud drowsily.

She lifted the heavy wooden bar and pushed open the weathered old barn door. The warm smell of cows and dung greeted her. The stumbling of hooves could be heard as the cows gradually got up, back end first, onto their legs. They were preparing for their daily milking ritual. A lowing came from Crabby, as if to say her udder was near to bursting.

'Poor old thing', smiled Mary Jane to herself. She patted the back of the brown and white cow fondly, before tying her to the barn wall and fetching her three-legged wooden stool. Soon the rhythmic sound of milk drumming into the tin bucket could be heard, amidst the snuffing of the cows at their bedding and their gentle breathing.

As she sat milking, her head pressed against Crabby's warm flank, she thought back to the day before. It had just been a normal day, milking the cows and later helping in the house, doing domestic tasks to help Sarah who was getting a bit old and creaky to tell the truth. They had been churning butter in the echoing dairy with its slate slabs, when Sarah had come out with some local gossip about the navvies who had come to work and live in Egloskerry.

'Tes said there's been trouble at the Simcoe Arms maid,' Sarah's usual loud voice was hushed, for gossip was not encouraged among the workers at Badharlick. 'Tes they navvies again so tis said, fighting and getting as drunk as Lords!'

Mary Jane had stopped her churning and pushed back a strand of cut auburn hair, touched with copper and golden glints where the sunlight shone on it, tucking it into her linen cap. She did not like the navvies very much, for somehow they had changed the atmosphere in her home village of Egloskerry into something darker, something not to be trusted.

She had sighed, thinking of the gang of young men who had been hanging about outside the village inn recently. It was uncomfortable walking past, she knew that from experience. They spoke in strange voices in accents which she found difficult to understand. But you would have to be stupid not to understand some of their lewd shouts as she walked past with her friend Ann on their way to the parish church for instruction in the Scriptures. Of course the public house was not open for the sale of 'the demon drink' on the Sabbath, so at least then walking to the church dedicated to St. Keri for both Morning and Evening Prayer felt considerably safer. The Methodist chapel-going farmers and their families had washed their hands of the whole situation in disgust.

'They d'say that someone punched the brother of the landlord after an argument, and t'was like all hell broke loose!' Sarah had shaken her old head in dismay that their peaceful little village, Egloskerry, should come to this depraved way of life. 'That old railway them are building in the Kensey valley has a lot to answer for. You mark my words, maid.' She shook her head once more. 'There'll be more trouble yet.'

The two of them had carried on with the butter-churning in silence, both of their minds full of the recent riotous happenings in the parish.

Later, up in her tiny room in the rafters of the farmhouse, Mary Jane had pondered over the excitement the railway would bring them. Well, so they had been told when they had all squeezed together for a meeting in the village hall back in the spring. Visions of far-away places, perhaps even the possibility of visits to the sea-side, had carried them all away in their minds from the drudgery of every-day life. How the people had listened, open-mouthed, when the railway engineers had painted a vivid picture of a glowing future for them all. Talk of railway engines and rolling stock, tunnelling and viaducts, had befuddled many of the older parishioners. Then some of the local farmers had started to grasp the reality, that railway lines may have to be built across their land, and the grumbling started. But more talk of something the men called 'compensation' seemed to smooth things over and the more argumentative farmers had subsided somewhat, minds quickly turning to dreams of imaginary fat profits when they took their cattle by train to market in Launceston, in the not-too-distant future.

Mary Jane climbed into her narrow bed and blew out the candle. Sarah could be heard deeply snoring in the next tiny room where the rafters had made an easy divide to accommodate the women-servants. But Mary Jane's mind, so usually placid, was full of people and pictures that night as she shivered below the blankets.

Moonlight filtered through the small window slit, catching the cracked mirror on the wooden box where her clothes were stored. She wondered how her family was, living up the road from the village near Penheale Manor. She missed her younger brothers and sisters, but she knew she should be grateful to live in, like the other farm servants, at Badharlick. She would see her family on Sunday at church no doubt.

Into the images of family came another face. A young man's face, with mesmerising dark eyes. She had felt something special happening when he had smiled at her at the village fair in the summer. Dear William... He was the only son of a nearby farmer, up towards Tregeare somewhere. Somewhere near Tregeare Green, he had told her but then, she had never actually been there for there had never been the need and it was a few miles probably. Perhaps she would walk out that way one day.

With this comforting thought and her tired body feeling much warmer, probably at the thought of that handsome William, Mary Jane closed her eyes. Soon her gentle breathing became more regular and she fell asleep, against a backdrop of Sarah's snores in the next room.

Chapter 3

The scene in Launceston on market day was a frantically busy one. The town's square was a seething mass of people, jostling one another on the cobbles, while the farmers' wives did brisk business in the Butter Market. The noise of the crowds was quite overwhelming, horses whinnying, cattle bellowing in distress, geese cackling and above all the shouts of the drovers and the auctioneers on their boxes amidst the pens.

Two young gentlewomen dressed in some style, walked side by side, pausing outside the magnificent doorway of the freshly-painted White Hart Hotel. They were only too aware of the inquisitive looks they had been getting from some of the younger men in the square, and their cheeks flushed at a particularly ribald comment from a gathering of loud drovers on the corner. A languid-looking gentleman sauntered behind them, looking in the window of the gentlemen's outfitters, and seeming to ignore the lewd remarks aimed at his sister and her friend.

Miss Elizabeth King knew only too well that she turned heads, for she was quite simply beautiful. Even as a child she had become used to being told that she was 'the prettiest girl ever' by her adoring father. Her eyes were intensely blue and her pale, silvery-blonde hair made her almost like a china doll in appearance. Then there were her stylish clothes, which stood out as remarkable in the Cornish market town of Launceston, but were worn by all girls of her class in society. She liked the fact that everyone turned their heads when she came into church at Laneast on Sunday mornings, sitting in the front in the family pew. She could feel their eyes on her throughout the service, particularly while the vicar (who also happened to be her ancient uncle), droned on and on in his lengthy sermon above them in the pulpit.

Elizabeth's female companion was as different from her as chalk and cheese, as they say. Her hair was as black as a raven's wing and it tumbled down in untamed curls and wild ringlets beneath her hat which looked as if she'd slung it on carelessly. Her clothes were not quite so fashionable, yet still very different in quality and style from the attire of the local young women and girls of Launceston (who changed outfits by simply putting on a clean apron and perhaps threading a new ribbon in their caps). On closer inspection the young woman's eyes were dark and lustrous, set against her olive-coloured skin. This then was Katherine, or Kate as she was known, as dark as Elizabeth was fair. If Elizabeth was a blue-eyed china doll in appearance, Kate was exotic-looking, perhaps like an Egyptian or from some other far-off land.

The young women waited patiently for a few minutes by the White Hart's ancient doorway, a huge Norman granite carved piece said to have come from the Priory or perhaps even the castle itself which loomed over the town square.

Elizabeth was not really used to waiting for anyone, let alone her brother who was still peering attentively in a shop window at the gentlemen's jackets and hats on display.

'Do come on Jasper!' her querulous voice carried along the pavement, while her companion Kate seemed content to watch the doings of the busy market with her lovely dark eyes.

Jasper sauntered towards his sister. It would not do to seem too hurried. Especially as he wanted to impress her rather lovely friend with his cool, detachment. Kate, it seemed, was staying at nearby

Werrington Park with distant family and Jasper found himself surprisingly taken with her dark, sultry looks.

'I think we should adjourn to the White Hart for some refreshment rather than loiter outside here on the pavement,' Jasper offered both arms to help them up the steps in their long dresses, 'Shall we ladies?'

Elizabeth frowned at her brother, disgruntled, for he was the loiterer, not them. She was a spoilt individual as Kate had quickly begun to realise and reluctantly she dragged her attention away from the market scene, with all its colour and noise. She was conscious of the young man's intense gaze, but took his arm in friendly fashion and the three of them entered the busy hotel.

'People say it's been as busy as this ever since the railway came to Launceston,' Jasper explained over a luncheon of excellent roast beef. He lifted his glass of red wine to his lips and studied Kate coolly over its rim. She felt his eyes on her and his obvious interest. Elizabeth seemed oblivious, fiddling with her new lace gloves on the tablecloth, for she only seemed to be interested when she herself took centre stage.

'And when will the railway continue westwards?' Kate asked, toying with the last roast potato on her plate, shifting it to and fro with no intentions of ever eating it. She put her knife and fork down and looked boldly at Jasper across the expanse of white linen tablecloth.

'The navvies are working on the deep cuttings along the Kensey valley now I believe, and some of the men are building bridges.' Jasper smiled, 'but when the next section to Egloskerry will actually be built and ready for use is anybody's guess.' He took a large swig at his wineglass and Kate heard him swallow loudly.

'Well quite honestly I can't wait,' Elizabeth joined the conversation, her gloves momentarily forgotten. 'I shall love being able to get a train from Egloskerry to Launceston instead of being jolted the whole way from Tregeare by old Ned in the carriage. It will make shopping for hats and finery so much easier.' She sighed and glanced down despairingly at her white, workless hands in her lap. 'These men you're talking about, these so-called navvies; they obviously need to work a lot harder and put in more hours it seems to me.'

Kate felt her colour rise. What on earth was she doing in the company of such a spoilt young woman? She felt quite simply like throwing that last potato across the table at Miss Elizabeth King and hitting her with it, hard! Elizabeth was just so unfeeling, so totally insensitive to the lives of others. These men she was referring to, probably grafted long hours in difficult conditions.

Jasper sensed the animosity and attempted to diffuse the situation. The last thing he wanted was for the two girls to fall out, as he was fascinated by this unusual dark-haired beauty smouldering opposite him.

'Well let's try and forget the railway for a while and indulge in some dessert … I would recommend the apple pie and cream. The cream's so thick you cut it with a knife!' Jasper smiled at Kate, ignoring his infuriating sister who seemed quite oblivious that anything she had said was out of order in any way.

After an uneasy lunch the group appeared out of the White Hart into the sunshine. The market was still going with a swing, butter and cheese and chickens being sold, but the main business of buying and selling cattle was over for the day. Many of the cows had been bought and were now plodding along the lanes, being driven back to the fields of their new owners, drovers slapping them on their rumps to make them move faster. The square was full of dirty straw and filth. Elizabeth held a tiny handkerchief over her nose, appalled at the country smell.

Kate took a sideways look at her and could not help but smile mischievously.

'I thought you lived out in the country Elizabeth?' You should be used to the smell of cows' shit!'

The last thing Kate saw as she lifted her skirts to climb into the waiting trap from Werrington Park was Elizabeth's horrified expression. But Jasper's stare was a mixture of fleeting surprise and total admiration.

Chapter 4.

On the very same day that Kate Polglaze had caused such offence to Elizabeth King outside the White Hart, the young man who had been beaten so badly on his way home from market the week before and left in a ditch to die, opened his eyes. His head hurt and his vision was blurred, but he could hear the comforting sound of old Annie's voice, and feel his mother's warm hand smoothing his brow.

'Tes all right William me ansum, twill all be fine now you'm awake once more,' Annie's voice wavered a bit, and she mopped her red-rimmed watery eyes with her apron.

He thought he must be back in his own bedroom, for surely that was the text on the wall opposite that his aunt had embroidered and framed for him. 'Love Thy Neighbour' it read and tiny violets adorned each corner. William closed his eyes again, wearily. Loving his neighbour never seemed a harder task. All he could remember was unbearable pain, the sound of unrecognizable men's voices and the thud of the violent blows being rained down on him. Then he thought he remembered the welcome feeling of calm afterwards, the silvery moon-blanched tones shining down on him as he lay in a dark ditch. He had thought he was dying, for he felt so cold and there was a strange light. But somehow or other, he now found he was back at his own home in his own bed.

'How long have I been laid up here Mother?' A weak voice, barely recognizable as his own, asked huskily.

'Sssh now William, don't over-tax yourself my dear.' His mother continued to stroke his brow, just like the days when he was a small child.

'You've been lying here near on a week,' Annie butted in, ignoring the frown of William's mother, Joan. 'Twas that Farmer Davey over at Athill what found you. Lying in a ditch moaning yer head off, he said. Lucky fer you he had a cow calving that night, or it might hev been too late!' She shook her old head and wiped the tears yet again.

'Well William is here now and he's safe and sound,' Joan's voice clearly showed her irritation. 'Isn't there something you should be doing down in the kitchen Annie? Or out in the dairy?'

The womanservant made her exit as speedily as her ancient legs would carry her, leaving Joan by her son's bedside. She tidied the bedding around William, who just lay staring at the white-washed ceiling.

'Now you just close your eyes and get some rest my son. I'm sure your father will be in to see you later when he comes home from the market.' Joan opened the window a little to let some fresh air into the stuffy bedroom, for there was a fire burning in the tiny grate.

William was glad when his mother left. He heaved a sigh of relief and moved his aching legs under the bedcovers. His head was pounding like a drum and there was a sore place on his cheek. He felt around it gently with his finger-tips. What other injuries had he gained? It all seemed a blur, but he could remember one distinctive voice before he'd blacked out, a voice which was not a local one that was for sure.

He was determined to find out who his cowardly attackers were, but first he must get well, get his strength up once more. And that would not happen if he stayed in bed, being mollycoddled by old Annie and his mother.

A few miles down the winding lane was the little farming community of Badharlick. The farms and a water-mill had once belonged to the Lord of Penheale Manor and all the corn was ground there. The water-mill still remained, its wheel dripping incessantly, a reminder of former days. It was on one of these farms that Mary Jane Jenkin lived and worked for a family named Baron, which had once been a common name in the parish of Egloskerry. John Baron of Badharlick sounded quite grand Mary Jane thought, as she worked at her daily tasks out in the fields or with Sarah in the dairy. But there was nothing grand about her work in the muddy yard or in the cold slate-shelved dairy. She wrinkled up her nose at the milky pans and churns, which left a sour smell no matter how many times she washed it all down, or scrubbed the slate floor on hands and knees.

That morning one of the village boys had come with news, already a week or so late. William, her William as she liked to think him, had been attacked and badly beaten. She was sweeping out the large farmhouse kitchen with its scrubbed table and copper pans glinting over the fireplace, when the boy from Egloskerry regaled them with the latest news. Mary Jane's broom stopped dead and she went as pale as a white-washed wall. The boy from the village was enjoying his role as story-teller, embellishing the tale of the night-time attack at Athill so that it became even more of a nightmare than it really was. Each farm that he'd visited, he'd added another juicy description or dramatic happening, so that the tragic tale he told to them by the time he reached Badharlick could almost have come from the pen of writer Charles Dickens himself.

'So is the poor young man dead?' Sarah's wrinkled old hands flew to her mouth, her jaw had dropped in shock at the terrible news revealing an open mouth full of gaps where once teeth had been.

'Please say he isn't,' Mary Jane's voice was more of a strange wail than anything else. She dropped her broom and clutched the high-backed settle as if for support.

The boy preened a bit, enjoying keeping the women in a state of suspense. 'Well... '

'Well what?' Old Sarah was not a woman to be played with. 'You young good-for-nothing! Just you wait till I see yer father up at the village Post Office! What's happened to that there William Treglown from up Tregeare Green?' She advanced on the story-teller with real menace, grabbing a large metal ladle as a weapon from the table as she did so.

The boy, Sam, realised he might have gone too far. These women here at Badharlick were not to be trifled with, although the younger one, still clinging to the settle, looked as if she might faint away altogether at any minute.

He backed towards the door as he blurted out, 'They d'say William's ' 'ome and in 'is bed, 'ee ain't dead anyways!' Then Sam bolted out into the yard before that mad old one with no teeth could hit him with that heavy-looking ladle.

Mary Jane sank down onto the settle, her heart beating so fast and loud she thought even old Sarah could probably hear it. A thin film of perspiration had gathered over her top lip, like a dewy moustache.

'Thank the dear Lord that William is still alive,' Mary Jane whispered more to herself than to Sarah. The older woman had subsided somewhat, grumbling about the village youth of today and their lack of respect for anyone and anything, as she lay the heavy ladle back on the kitchen table.

Mary Jane's stomach felt like it had turned to water after that shock. It was not that anything had really gone on with William, after all she rarely saw him, but she could not forget the way he had looked at her at the village fete last summer. Those eyes of his had made her feel quite faint as he had watched her closely, laughing with her brothers and sisters in her sprigged, summery dress. Their eyes had met and a deep, embarrassing flush had spread over her face. Then he had been dragged away to join the Tug-o-war, where all the local young men could show off their muscles to the giggling village girls.

She snapped out of her day-dream, aware of Sarah's muttering and mumbling as she went about her daily chores.

'I'm going out the back to the privvy,' Mary Jane lifted her voice so she could be heard amidst the clattering of utensils in the kitchen.

Yes, that dark-eyed William had certainly had an effect on her, in more ways than she cared to mention!

Chapter 5.

Elizabeth King stood on the steps of Tregeare House, daydreaming in the late spring sunshine. The blooming rhododendrons were a mass of colour and before her was an immaculate broad sweeping lawn. In the distance was the brooding outline of Bodmin Moor. Mellow light reflected off her pale golden hair, which was topped by an elegant hat trimmed with dusky pink roses. Her cream day dress fell in soft cascades and Elizabeth sighed with happiness at her own perfect appearance, as Ned appeared with the carriage.

'Jasper! Ned is here... at last!' Her voice carried back into the entrance hall of the dazzling white Palladian mansion, as she pulled on yet another newly acquired pair of gloves.

Her brother appeared from the dark interior, screwing his eyes up at the bright sunlight. Jasper felt irritable, he had hardly slept the night before thinking about the dark beauty, Kate Polglaze. He was still angry with his sister Elizabeth – for all her spoilt ways and her seeming lack of any human understanding.

Now he had to accompany her to the musty church of St. Sidwell's for Morning Prayer, and that doddering old great-uncle of theirs, the Vicar of Laneast, would be up in the pulpit delivering his sermon for hours no doubt. By that time Jasper's back-side would be numb, the locals would be restive and the whole congregation would be sure that they were all steeped in sin and going straight to Hell! The only one who seemed to enjoy this part of the service was Elizabeth, as the farmers' wives would be admiring the trimmings on her new hat as she sat in the family pew. Jasper smirked to himself, thinking that the lusty farmers' sons would probably be dreaming of getting her on a pile of hay in the nearest barn and showing her what for, no doubt!

Jasper felt it would be not be quite as bad if their parents were at home with them, as Elizabeth was more bearable then, but his father was in far-off Plymouth on a few days of business. Their mother had accompanied him with the three younger children, so they were probably strolling on the Hoe in the sunshine watching the ships and boats, enjoying the maritime scene.

The journey to the church was uneventful, Ned driving the family carriage with its pair of glossy horses, their coats gleaming after a good grooming by the stable lads who had been up since the crack of dawn. Elizabeth was looking forward to the adulation of the local girls who looked up to her as one of the most fashionable ladies of North Cornwall. That they did not actually like her as a person one bit, mattered not to Elizabeth. As far as she was concerned, they were really little more than peasants! They would bob a curtsey with lowered eyes as she entered the damp old church porch, and she relished that feeling of superiority, brushing past them and barely nodding as her only reply.

As Jasper had expected, the sermon was long and extremely dreary, his elderly uncle droning on interminably in the pulpit, as if he relished his power to keep the increasingly fidgety congregation in their uncomfortable wooden pews. But it gave Jasper time to think, of how he could engineer another meeting with Kate Polglaze who was residing temporarily with family at Werrington Park. But for how long? His mind was all over the place and he suddenly realised that the sermon had ended and everyone was on their feet rustling the pages of their prayer books. He glanced at his sister Elizabeth, whose doll-like face betrayed no flicker of emotion whatsoever. What went on in that empty head of hers, he wondered, not for the first time.

The vicar's long-winded prayers followed the creed, and included the usual ones for peace, the health of Queen Victoria and for the poor and the sick of the parish. The final prayer was for a man who had been severely injured whilst undertaking dangerous work with explosives whilst working on constructing the railway. But the name was not a local one and anyway he was working on the border with Egloskerry parish. Many folk shook their heads at the mere mention of that darned old railway, which seemed to bring a trail of death and destruction to their part of the world, tucked away quietly on their farms and cottages in rural North Cornwall.

The warmth of the sunshine was very welcome as they left the gloom of the church porch, where a gaggle of girls in their Sunday best whispered as Jasper walked past, his sister on his arm. The ancient vicar was already outside, politely nodding his white head as he listened and responded to the conversation of the more prosperous local farmers and their bonneted wives.

'Seems like there's been a nasty accident on the railway construction site then vicar,' the booming voice of the local auctioneer and cattle dealer, Trewhella, could be heard clearly across the churchyard, with its mossy old gravestones.

'Unfortunately so, Mr. Trewhella,' the vicar sighed and shook his head sadly. 'The poor young man has been blinded and lost his arm it seems. Working on constructing the railway from Launceston can be a dangerous enterprise. He's been taken to the Infirmary, but I fear that little can be done to restore him to his former self.'

'Damned railway! Brings nothing but damned trouble to these parts, pardon my language Vicar!' A short man with a bulbous nose joined in the conversation.

'Well we must all look to the future you know,' the incumbent gently reminded them, searching vainly among his parishioners for someone who would not want to moan to him about the railway.

A vision of loveliness in cream and pink roses appeared on his left. It was his great-niece, Elizabeth, accompanied by her brother Jasper.

'Ah Elizabeth,' the vicar smiled benignly, 'and Jasper too, of course. Well and how is life at Tregeare House these days?'

Elizabeth King smiled sweetly at the old man, 'Wonderful Great-Uncle! The rododendrons are out, the sun is shining and we have not a care in the world.'

Just at that very moment the large family of a tied farm-worker filed past them along the churchyard path, in clothes decidedly worn and patched yet scrupulously clean. The father touched his forelock to Jasper King the young squire-to-be and Miss Elizabeth, while his gaunt-looking wife bobbed a pathetic curtsey and a string of young daughters in drab grey attire stared wide-eyed at Elizabeth's beautiful dress and rose-trimmed hat.

In that moment Jasper seemed to sense the awful difference in circumstances and he took his sister's arm, saying, 'You really must pay us a visit soon at Tregeare, Uncle. But we must go, I can see Ned waiting with the carriage.'

Elizabeth was nettled as Ned helped her into the carriage. 'Why did you rush me away like that Jasper? You are so infuriating at times! I did not get the chance for the womenfolk to admire my new hat and dress as we stood outside the church porch!'

'For God's sake Elizabeth, just for once stop thinking about yourself,' spat Jasper angrily at his spoilt sister. 'Didn't you see that family dressed in near rags while we were talking to Uncle?' He took a deep breath, 'And come to that, didn't you hear the awful news about that young man injured by explosives while constructing the railway?'

Elizabeth looked at her brother with disbelief, 'And that is all my fault is it? I expect he was one of those dreadful navvies we all keep hearing about. Ruffians the lot of them!' Elizabeth smoothed the folds of her dress and looked away from her seemingly irate brother at the green fields lush in the sunshine.

'So you won't want to ride in the train carriages when the line from Launceston is extended then?' Jasper glared at her. 'The railway won't build itself Elizabeth!'

An uneasy silence all the way home to Tregeare had ruined the morning and not even the delicious roast lamb and a few glasses of the best red wine from the cellar could pacify Jasper. In the afternoon he called for his hunter to be saddled and rode up onto Tregeare Down to blow the cobwebs away.

Why was he feeling so angry with the world? He just knew that at times he could simply strangle his sister Elizabeth. But the picture which kept forming in the back of his mind was not his sister's blank china-doll blue eyes, but a pair of dark eyes and black unruly hair. Both of these features belonged to the rather exotic-looking Kate Polglaze, currently residing at the estate at Werrington Park.

Chapter 6.

That Sunday when Jasper was cantering over Laneast Down with his mind full of a woman with tousled black hair, that same woman, Kate Polglaze, was walking in the beautiful gardens at Werrington Park. She had been to church at Werrington that morning with her Aunt Nell with whom she was staying, and received Holy Communion. After a quiet lunch with her aunt, her beefy, red-faced uncle and even beefier-looking cousin Jack, she was feeling extremely bored and cooped up. Their talk was all about cattle and crops, which her thin, rather worn out aunt seemed used to. Outside the sun was shining through the latticed windows, enticing Kate to leave the confines of the well-built farmhouse to walk in the lovely gardens of Werrington House itself.

Kate had been staying with her mother's sister for some six weeks or so, while her mother was recovering from the birth of yet another late baby to add to her large brood. This time things had gone dreadfully wrong and the tiny baby had died. The family doctor had strongly advised her mother not to have any further additions to the family and Kate's father had quite simply gone red in the face with embarrassment and blustered away at the doctor in his usual gruff fashion.

'She's worn out Mr. Polglaze, there's nothing more to be said.' The doctor had packed his shabby black leather bag. 'Another child may even be the death of her!' He had mounted his patient cob, touched his hat to Polglaze, and trotted off down the driveway.

Kate had been packed off from her home at Caerhays to stay with Aunt Nell, and to be honest she was glad of the change of scene. She was sick of babies and children running riot at home.

The tranquillity of life at Werrington was like a dream come true, even though she was not actually one of the 'real family' from the Big House, as she constantly reminded herself. She was a step up above the local girls, but certainly not on quite the same level as the descendants of the Duke of Northumberland or even that of Miss Elizabeth King of Tregeare. Not that she had been impressed with the behaviour of that spoilt creature at Launceston market. They had been pretty much thrown together by her aunt, who was distantly related to the Kings by marriage.

Now Kate smiled to herself as she remembered her parting shot to Elizabeth about the smell of cows shit! She remembered the horrified expression on that china-doll face, and the admiration of her rather good-looking brother, Jasper. Yes he was good-looking Kate admitted, and there was something about him which had impressed her. He had seemed somewhat languid and detached at first, but over lunch in the White Hart she had slightly warmed to him. It was obvious that he had become impatient with his sister, particularly in their brief discussion about the railway.

The railway seemed to rouse all sorts of passions in the Launceston area. It had certainly modernised the town and its market, her uncle had explained over many recent dinners. Now some of the cattle could even be brought in on Tuesdays in railway trucks before being driven up the long meandering road from the station, instead of drovers bringing the livestock miles and miles along back country lanes. Yes there were those small farmers who stuck to the old methods and of course the railway line had yet to be extended west beyond Launceston itself. Then it would open up whole new worlds to the people of North Cornwall. Uncle Tom had undone the buttons on his waistcoat, stuck his pipe back in his mouth with an air of total satisfaction and puffed away peacefully.

But Kate had soon come to realise that the railway was not perceived to be a good thing by everyone. That was because of the lewd behaviour of the so-called 'navvies' who were working on it. It seemed that these men had somehow changed things in the area, partly due to their large numbers. They were certainly different to the placid local men who were mostly farmers and shopkeepers. These 'navvies' looked and acted tough and they spoke in strange accents. They had a reputation that they worked hard and they played hard. Some of them had apparently built bridges over rivers in far-off places like Cardiff, and now they had arrived in what they thought to be a backwater in Cornwall, which was full of dull farmworkers and simple country girls.

Kate sat down on a wrought-iron seat, took off her annoying Sunday hat and turned her face up to the warmth of the May sunshine. It was so lovely here, the grounds of the Big House as she called it, were smooth, well cared for lawns. It was a luxury to have time to walk in the gardens without a brood of younger brothers and sisters to constantly minister to. Yet she had a niggling feeling that she needed to be doing something. Something more useful, something to fill her life. She could not imagine a daily routine like Elizabeth King's, constantly dressing herself up and flaunting her new outfits in a quest to look perfect at all times. Kate knew that her own clothes were stylish, but not the very latest fashion. There was more to life than that, she mused. But she certainly did not want a life like her own mother's, producing a long line of babies until she was simply worn out. There must be something else. Something more challenging. Not for the first time she thought it must be more interesting to be a man, with more freedom to choose your path in life. She was a determined young woman and Kate knew she wanted to do something exceptional in her life, something that would make a difference to others.

She picked up her hated Sunday hat and stood up with new resolve. All around her were the stunning gardens full of spring flowers and shrubs, while below the lawns in the tranquil valley was the river meandering in the pastures full of cattle which were grazing peacefully. High up above the mass of dark trees on the distant skyline, a buzzard wheeled in slow circles, screeching its distinctive call.

On her return to the farmhouse, she realised something was wrong. Hens scattered in all directions and something, someone, was lying on the cobbled area by the open back door. Her cousin Jack was kneeling on the ground, his broad, bullock-like shoulders blocking her view. She could see her Aunt Nell, also on her knees, hands up to her mouth, rocking to and fro. A strange, unearthly mewing sound seemed to be coming from her.

Kate quickly reached them and there on the cobbles lay Uncle Tom, his face twisted with pain clutching his chest. She could see that her aunt seemed a hopeless case, but Jack did at least look of some use, even if his face was beetroot-red as he repeatedly said, 'Feyther! Feyther, look up at me. Open yer eyes Feyther!'

Kate firmly moved her aunt out of the way and told her clearly to tell a stable boy to fetch the doctor from nearby Ladycross. Her aunt nodded bleakly, her eyes betraying her fear. But she scuttled over the yard towards the stables, like a worried hen.

Then Kate turned her attention to her uncle and her jabbering cousin, Jack. She felt calm, strong in the face of sudden adversity.

She undid Uncle Tom's collar-studs around his neck and loosened his tight leather belt, talking to him soothingly all the while, calming him. His eyes were closed now and he was making guttural sounds deep in his throat. His forehead was clammy with a cold sweat. Jack knelt back helplessly on his heels, his huge hands like hams shaking uncontrollably. He was only too glad to let someone else take over responsibility, even if it was his cousin Kate who he did not even like that much with all her strong, modern views and different ways from down in Caerhays.

'Tis like a bleddy vice round my chest maid,' Uncle Tom's voice, a hoarse whisper, could barely be heard. The agonising pain simply exhausted him.

Again Kate soothed him, talking gently, telling him the doctor was on his way and he must keep calm. She sent Jack for a piece of dampened flannel so that she could apply it to his father's forehead which was sweating copiously now.

At long last the aptly-named Doctor Blood appeared on horseback in the yard, amidst a cloud of dust. A gaggle of housemaids from the Big House were walking in the lane and they stopped as they saw him cantering past on his sweating mare. They were pressed against the hedge and frozen to the spot, knowing something was obviously wrong at the farm. What was the emergency? Who could it be?

Perhaps Jack, the farmer's son, had been kicked in the head by a horse! Or perhaps something had happened to the frail, mousy farmer's wife who was well-known to suffer from her nerves.

The maids picked up their best Sunday skirts, held onto their hats and began to run quickly back up the lane towards Werrington House. They took a risk for once and ran across the smooth lawns where a carefree Kate had ambled earlier that same afternoon. The excitable housemaids all had a feeling that when the latest news eventually came through from Home Farm, it would not be good!

Chapter 7.

A week had passed since the happenings at the farm in Werrington. Kate's uncle had lingered on in the Infirmary at Launceston, his once-strong body, weathered over the years by sun and wind, lay under glacial white sheets. A strange smell of iodine and rubber greeted them at the door when Kate had accompanied her aunt and Jack on their visit. Uncle Tom seemed to have shrunk somehow, lying low in the single bed. Jack stared at the bleached white tiles on the walls above the bed, twisting his hat in his hands, much roughened from hard physical work. He did not know what to do or say to his father, who had changed beyond all recognition in such a short space of time. Aunt Nell wept silently on a wooden chair, while her husband puffed out his lips with his laboured breathing and the rattle in his throat went on and on.

There was one other patient lying flat in a bed at the other end of the long, bleak room. Kate could see an occasional movement there, a heavily-bandaged hand was lifted up to an even more bandaged head now and then, accompanied by soft groaning. Brisk footsteps came into the room. A starched nurse appeared with a tray and placed it on a table nearby. She helped the patient, a man it appeared to be, to sit up more propped by pillows. Then she proceeded to feed him with some soup, speaking to him curtly for he turned his head to one side.

'I haven't got time to waste on trying to feed you if you are going to be difficult young man!' The nurse's voice was clipped and as cold as ice.

Kate longed to go over and help, again there was that overwhelming need to be useful, rather than just sit in silence feeling useless by the bedside of her dying uncle.

Jack nudged her and whispered rather too loudly, 'I do b'leeve tis the poor chap who was working over Egloskerry way on one of they railway cuttings. They d'say he were badly injured in an explosion.'

Kate glanced quickly over at the continuing attempt at soup-feeding, over at the other sick-bed.

Sighing heavily Jack continued, 'T'other night at bell-ringing practice, someone reckoned he've been blinded.' He paused gloomily, 'An' if that edn't bad enough, he've lost an arm too!'

There was a sudden crash from the other bed as the soup bowl hit the floor and an exclamation from the nurse who had jumped to her feet with alacrity. 'That's done it now. A nourishing bowl of soup, completely wasted. Just look at the mess you've made!'

A muffled swearing could be heard, so that Aunt Nell stopped her weeping in shock and horror. Jack stared in disbelief. You never even heard swearing like that in the Bell Inn on market day! But worse was to come.

The soup-covered nurse was wiping herself down with a cloth and she marched angrily out of the room, her shoes making a loud staccato amidst the quiet of the sick and dying.

Uncle Tom's eyes flickered briefly and shut again. The terrible groaning from the other bed resumed, like some poor beast going to the slaughterhouse.

Kate took a deep breath and stood up. It was time for some kind of action on her part. She looked at her aunt perched on the edge of a hospital chair like she was made of porcelain; she had resumed her silent weeping. Cousin Jack was lumped on his tiny chair like a bullock on a milk-stand, staring at her sudden movement with his blank blue eyes.

She made her way to the other bed and stood looking at the devastation. Soup everywhere, looking like faded blood on the snow-white-sheets. A man lying in the bed, swathed in bandages so he could not see. He was groaning with the pain and Kate could see that he had an arm missing. Jack was right then, this seemed to be the young man so badly injured in the explosion on the railway cutting.

Kate smiled at him, not that he could see her, and said something to him softly. She laid a comforting hand on his remaining good hand and spoke to him again. He turned his throbbing head towards her as if vaguely aware of a presence at his bedside.

'I've got the worst bloody headache I've ever had,' he muttered desperately. 'Wheer am I? Have I been in an accident? What the bloody 'ell is the matter with me?'

Tears came to Kate's eyes, but she quickly brushed them away. She still held his hand and squeezed it warmly.

'You're safe in the Infirmary at Launceston,' she said in a low voice.

'I can't remember what happened,' the man murmured. 'There was a loud noise and terrible pain in my head.' He stopped. 'I thought I was dying...'

'No you are not dying,' Kate spoke kindly, softly. 'But you have injuries. You have been cleaned up here in the Infirmary by the doctor and the nurses.'

The door opened and a man in black with a droopy moustache, a doctor, entered the echoing room. He stopped, looked up from the sheaf of papers in his hand and frowned. Kate stood up straight, for she had been bending over the injured man's bed. She gently relinquished her hold on his good hand.

'Don't go, don't bloody well leave me,' came a desperate plea from the bed. You're like an Angel, come to look after me.'

Kate glanced over at her aunt on her wooden chair, oblivious of anything but the dying man in front of her. Jack stared back at Kate blankly.

'Young man, this kind lady has her own relatives to attend to,' said the doctor briskly. The young man lay back on his pillows, his head throbbing. He was near to tears for he needed someone to cling to in this painful new world that he did not really understand. 'Now I'm going to have a close look at your wounds and we'll see how...' the doctor's voice dropped as he pulled a screen around the bed.

Kate walked sadly and quietly across the room to her Uncle Tom's bed. Her aunt seemed lost in another world, but it was Jack's face which alarmed her. His ruddy cheeks had turned the colour of lard.

It was then she realised that the terrible rasping breathing of her uncle had stopped, for Uncle Tom was dead.

Chapter 8.

The lanes around Egloskerry were dressed in their May plumage of fresh green, froths of cow-parsley, pink campion, bluebells and buttercups. Wild garlic grew in abundance down by the ford over the stream, its distinct smell mixed with the oily tang of sheepswool from the flock of ewes and lambs grazing in a nearby pasture.

Mary Jane Jenkin took a deep breath and closed her eyes. It was quite simply a beautiful May morning and, to cap it all, she had a rare day off from her labours at Badharlick. Well most of a day off, for she had risen early to do the milking, but she was now free of chores for a few precious hours.

While milking Crabby and listening to the satisfying spurts of milk in the pail, she had decided to pay a surprise visit to her family at home. Killicoff, was one of a row of three agricultural cottages, opposite the pretty gatehouse to Penheale Manor. Old Sarah had been up early too, baking, and she had checked the kitchen was empty of prying eyes before giving Mary Jane a fresh loaf of bread to take to her mother and a few freshly-laid brown eggs for the growing family of children. These were now in a small wicker basket, covered with a clean cotton napkin. Mary Jane knew that her mother would be delighted with this simple gift, for times were hard at Killicoff.

As she walked down towards the river where three lanes joined, her thoughts wandered to William whose family lived a few miles up in the other direction at Tregeare Green. Was he lying abed? Or was he getting any better after the violent assault on him? No news had reached Badharlick since Sam Strike had arrived in the kitchen with his dramatic tales which had brought the fear of God into her mind and made Sarah threaten him with a heavy ladle! In fact news had been in short supply, except for a horrible story of an explosion somewhere in the valley where gangs of men were working on the railway cuttings. That had made old Sarah shake her head and strongly blaspheme like Mary Jane had never heard her before, for she was vehemently against anything to do with the extending of the railway track to Egloskerry.

'Why do we need an iron horse out here at 'Skerry?' she'd moaned, after she had calmed down from her outburst and was sitting on the settle by the hearth. 'We'm all right like we be... Tis nothing but the devil's work in our midst.' And she'd rocked to and fro muttering, while Mary Jane had tidied up around her.

All these things were going through her mind as she turned left at the weathered sign towards the village of Egloskerry. Birds were singing and a wren went skittering through the hedgerow busily. A blackbird sang loudly on the branch of a nearby beech tree as she made her way up the lane. On her right was a fairly flat piece of pasture-land. She thought she remembered overhearing a man, not a local man but one in a dark suit with a gold chain hanging from his waistcoat, talking about the land in an animated fashion to some of the farmers from the parish at the meeting in the village hall about the railway.

'It would be an ideal piece of land for a station for Egloskerry, if it ever comes to that in the future.' The farmers had looked at each other with raised eyebrows and much shaking of heads. It all seemed a dream to them. They dealt in cattle and sheep, crops and pasture. Not in the building of railway stations here in isolated Egloskerry! The man had fiddled with his heavy chain and brought out a gold watch which he then consulted, as if to say it could all be achieved within the next five minutes or so.

Mary Jane's friend Eliza had whispered scornfully, 'He'm just showing off his gold watch for us all to see. There won't never be a railway station built 'ere in Egloskerry maid.' She had tossed her abundant hair back like a filly, 'And I d'know, for Father told me.' She had nodded her young head sagely, for her father was the oracle as far as she was concerned.

Mary Jane approached the straggling cottages near the school and the sound of a horse's hoofs could be plainly heard. Around the next corner came a man clothed in plain black on a dappled grey mare, the vicar of Egloskerry. He was on his way to visit the old and sick of his parish and on seeing Mary Jane he pulled on his reins and the mare gladly stopped for a moment and proceeded to snatch mouthfuls of greenery from the hedgerow.

'So you're on your way home to Killicoff I take it, Mary Jane,' the voice was refined but there was a gentle tone with it. 'How do you like the new arrangements that have taken place with your family? I'm sure it will all be very useful in these times of hardship.'

It was quite obvious by the girl's expression that she was mystified by this remark. The horse was champing on its bit and she took a pace back, away from the restless hooves.

'I don't know what you mean sir,' Mary Jane bobbed a clumsy half-curtsey, not liking the way the huge mare was now rolling its eyes at her.

'Well Mary Jane, I'll let your parents tell you the good news then,' the vicar bowed his head towards her in its faded black hat. 'Life at Killicoff will never be the same again, you know.' He picked up the reins, gave the mare a gentle nudge with his dusty boots, and they continued clip-clopping down the leafy lane.

When she got near the Post Office and shop, Mary Jane stopped to think. Should she go in to buy a bag of sweets as a small treat for her brothers and sisters to share? If so, she may hear some news about William Treglown, who was never far from her mind these days. That thought strengthened her resolve, for how else was she to find out if he was on the road to recovery or lying in a darkened sick-room at Tregeare Green?

The bell tinkled as she opened the door and there was the familiar smell of paper and ink, polish, spices and tobacco all mixed together as she stepped inside. Voices stopped dead as she entered. Two women stared towards the door to check who it was, before they could continue the latest village gossip. The postmistress appeared from behind a teetering pile of brown paper parcels and peered at her over her spectacles.

'Oh it's you Mary Jane!' The post mistress glanced up at her and took off her spectacles to see better. 'I expect you're on your way to see what's happening at Killicoff nowadays.'

One of the women, who looked rather gaunt and pale, sniffed loudly and looked down her long nose. The other, a rotund farmer's wife adorned with a squashed bonnet and a voluminous apron, smiled encouragingly hoping for a story to follow.

'Well I'm just visiting home as usual Miss Paul.' Mary Jane smiled sweetly back at the smiling farmer's wife who she knew was a great chapel-goer. 'Can I have a bag of your Bullseyes please?'

There was an awkward silence as the sweets were weighed out and tipped into a sliver of paper. Mary Jane handed over a few coins and beat a hasty retreat outside. As the bell tinkled once more and she shut the door firmly behind her, she could imagine the conversation already re-starting in the dark confines of the Post Office. That was the trouble in a small village, by the afternoon most people knew the gossip, including who had posted a letter and to whom.

At tiny Church Cottage next door, an old lady was peering past her lace-edged curtains at anyone who passed. 'Morning Mrs. Gynn,' Mary Jane raised a hand in a wave. A sad-eyed spaniel looked out through the gate and wagged his tail momentarily.

What on earth was happening at home? She knew that it was the talk of Egloskerry and she hoped that it did not involve yet another baby on its way. No, it was more than that, it must be something out of the ordinary. But what?

As she walked along the road leading to Penheale Manor, her mind was so full of different happenings that she quite forgot to avoid the place in the overgrown hedgerow where the weasels were. Slouching footsteps coming towards her made her look up, escaping from her reverie.

It was a young man, a stranger to Mary Jane, dark and strong-looking in a working man's attire of thick trousers, white shirt and waistcoat with a brightly-coloured kerchief round his neck. As he passed by, he seemed almost to wink his eye at her and he smiled, showing a set of very white teeth against his swarthy skin. Then he continued along the road to the village whistling tunelessly as he went, his canvas crib bag swinging in his work-roughened hand.

He had winked at a country girl with pretty golden and copper-coloured hair, nothing more, so it was soon out of his mind.

Mary Jane turned in at the gateway to Killicoff and saw a face quickly disappear from one of the windows. Out by the pump was an empty bucket and the slate steps were glistening with the clean water sloshed on them in the sunlight. The water was always cold and clear. Chickens moped and scratched in the garden up by the rows of growing vegetables, near the pigsty and the privvy which was camouflaged between two hedges. It all looked like home, the same as ever.

Her mother appeared in the doorway wiping her reddened hands on her coarse work apron. Two small children clung to her skirts, one with his thumb stuck in his mouth.

'Mary Jane! We didn't expect you dear,' taking her daughter in a warm embrace. 'Come on in. So much has happened in the last few days!'

She followed her mother into the large living room, dominated by the range where the kettle steamed amidst pots and pans. The children clutched at Mary Jane now demanding their sister's attention, as she put her basket on the table with its oil lamp and sat down on the settle by the open door. There was a wonderful aroma of newly-baked saffron cake and her mother's usually tired face was wreathed with smiles.

'Well Mother? What's been going on here that the whole village is talking about?' Mary Jane wrenched off her white cap and shook her tangled hair. The coppery gold glinted in the shafts of sunlight.

'Twas your father's idea and we thank God for the opportunity,' her mother paused nervously, looking at her eldest daughter's frowning face. 'We've taken in some lodgers here at Killicoff.' She twisted her apron anxiously.

'Lodgers? Here at home with our family?' This was not quite the news Mary Jane had expected to hear somehow. But then, she reflected, she hadn't known what on earth to expect.

'Twill help pay the bills dear,' her mother almost pleaded. 'It won't be forever.' She took a deep breath, 'They're all railway workers... navvies, and we've managed to squeeze in eleven of them.'

Chapter 9.

Jasper King rode into Launceston on market day with one thing on his mind, to hopefully bump into the delicious Kate Polglaze. He had not been able to get her out of his mind, so that morning he'd had his gleaming gelding saddled earlier than usual and made his getaway from Tregeare House before his sister Elizabeth came looking for him as her market day-chaperone. He stabled his horse at the Little White Hart and made his way through the busy streets to the cobbled square, where all the main business of the day took place. Rows of wagons were lined up as usual down by St. Mary's Church, some horses still standing between the shafts, their heads drooping with tiredness, the smell of horse dung overpowering.

There were people everywhere, leather-gaitered farmers and dealers heckling, buxom wives bartering in the Butter market, cattle crammed into pens, mournfully helving. The loud crowing of cockerels could be heard as they strutted their stuff for all to see, like country gentlemen resplendent in bright, colourful waistcoats. Jasper's eyes did not really take in the lively scene, for he was searching, searching for Kate's black unruly ringlets amidst the hats and bonnets, amidst the noise and confusion.

Suddenly his eyes focused on a ruddy-faced young drover he recognised from Werrington estate, who was standing by one of the cattle pens, aimlessly poking a stick through the bars at a disconsolate-looking heifer. Jasper made a beeline for him, and the drover jumped back guiltily as Jasper King, (one of them there wealthy Kings from Tregeare), seemed to want to start up a conversation with him of all people, about the family at Werrington Home Farm.

In very little time Jasper had managed to elicit some information from the rustic character about the recent events there. He had gleaned that Miss Kate Polglaze was (thankfully) still in residence, but there had been a terrible shock, a sudden death at the farm, none other than Kate's own uncle. The family was in deep mourning, it seemed. The funeral was yet to be held. A coin changed hands to the rustic's great surprise and he automatically touched his forelock, still with that bewildered look on his flushed face, for he knew only too well that Jasper King had a reputation locally for being a tight-fisted bugger.

Across the square Jasper could see his father Philip King, named after his illustrious ancestor Philip Gidley King, talking animatedly with a well-to-do farmer from nearby St. Stephen's on its hill across the valley. His father's normally stern features were lit up in intense discussion and he watched the two men shake hands as if on a deal and disappear through the Norman doorway into the White Hart.

Jasper would not be going there then, he thought to himself, even though it was his usual haunt on market days. His father would be critical about something no doubt, if they came face-to-face. Even if it was only to ask where his sister was and why he wasn't chaperoning her as was the assumed habit. Elizabeth was his father's favourite child, his pretty daughter of whom he was immensely proud. He had spoiled her rotten, giving her all the material possessions she wanted, making her the silly, thoughtless creature she had become. There had been times that Jasper had wanted to stand up and shout at his father that he must be blind not to see Elizabeth as she truly was, a simpering fool most of the time, with no concern for anyone but herself and the latest dresses and hats arriving from London on the train.

Maybe, he pondered, that was why he had become so quickly obsessed with Kate Polglaze. In their one encounter over lunch he had noticed signs of a depth of character often missing from the women he was introduced to in his parents' circle of friends and acquaintances. Kate did not seem to mind that her black hair was rather tousled, and that her dress was certainly not of the most up-to-date design. She had talked of the railway and its workers with a certain empathy and she had not minced her words with his sister, her parting shot, as she'd climbed into the waiting horse and trap, being about the country smell of cow shit!

He turned away from the bustle of the market square, avoiding a group of young men he would normally drink with, and made his solitary way through the crowds towards the Bell Inn instead. He needed a brandy and to think. How could he engineer another meeting with the sultry Kate? A couple of brandies later a smile appeared over his handsome features. That was it! He would attend the imminent funeral of Kate's uncle at Werrington and offer his condolences to the family, whilst ingratiating himself with Kate at the same time.

It was the morning of the funeral at St. Martin of Tours Church at Werrington. Most of the estate workers had been given permission to attend, indeed it was expected of them by those at the Big House. The men had scrubbed their faces, polished their boots and squeezed into tight collars and clean shirts. Now they looked suitably uncomfortable as they waited, in the churchyard. The women and serving-girls donned their Sunday best, all in solemn, inky black.

Jasper trotted past the many traps and gigs in the lane, only too aware of the keen looks of many locals. At breakfast that morning he had announced to his father that he would represent the King family at Tom Tremain's funeral, for after all the dead man's wife was a distant relative of their own family.

His father had frowned hard as always, but as he had no intentions of making the trek all the way over to Werrington himself for a mere farmer's funeral, he paused, then nodded curtly. He took a loud swig at his cup of tea and wiped his mouth with a pristine napkin, which he tossed carelessly on the table. He smelt a rat. Why would his normally indolent son want to ride all the way over to Werrington Park?

'Make sure you don't make a damned fool of yourself!' his father had growled, 'Remember you're a King when all is said and done.' He had stalked out of the sunlit room, leaving Jasper to finish a quietly jubilant breakfast in peace, for his mother was still upstairs in bed, as was Elizabeth, and the younger ones were being dealt with in the Nursery end of the house. He was thankful for that, especially as he could imagine his sister, Elizabeth, raising her eyebrows and very quickly putting two and two together.

And now he was being ushered into the damp, Gothic-looking church by an ancient man in stiff high collars, wheezing loudly, as if he was also about to embark on his last journey out of this world.

The coffin of Thomas Tremain would soon rest on the bare wooden supports in the chancel and the church was adorned with freshly cut flowers from Werrington House, formerly Manor. The church itself was packed with people mostly from the farming fraternity, with seats reserved at the side for members of the Williams family who were the guardians of the old manor itself yet spent most of their time it seemed at Caerhays Castle. These seats were soon filled, the women in the congregation craning their necks to see the hats of the ladies from the Big House, as they called it.

The sound of whispering and shuffling feet interspersed with a muffled sobbing came from the church porch. The family of Thomas Tremain had arrived, it seemed. The heavy coffin was borne in by six strong-looking farmer friends of the deceased, sweating as they struggled to get through the doorway. Jasper saw a blur of the vicar, followed by a huge oaf of a man with bewildered blue eyes (Cousin Jack) who was trying to support his mother, a thin, small woman clothed in sombre black. It was the widow who was making the unearthly sobbing. The Tremain family walked behind in strict order of precedence, but it was then he saw Kate Polglaze, holding the hand of a young pale-faced child.

Jasper sucked in his breath. She walked slowly past, oblivious to the sea of faces. How beautiful she looked in her solemn mourning, her wild black hair pinned up under a wide-brimmed hat, her lustrous dark eyes staring straight ahead.

And in that moment he knew he was lost.

Chapter 10

After the funeral there was a tea held at Home Farm, trestle tables covered in bleached white cloths, laden with cold meats and pasties, plates of saffron cake and jam and cream splits. Most of the estate workers soon made their way back to their daily tasks, glad to wrench off tight collars and boots and to escape from the claustrophobic atmosphere of mourning, and that feeling of never knowing quite what to say to the bereaved.

The family closed in. Kate was most attentive to her fragile-looking aunt, fetching a cup of tea and the tiniest of morsels on a plate to tempt her to eat. However Aunt Nell seemed dazed by the sense of occasion and the crowd of people, some whispering and making kind, sympathetic glances in her direction. She sat on the edge of a chair like a brittle piece of bone china, about to fall and crack.

The men were much more relaxed, eating ravenously from the funeral spread. Jack had lost that bewildered look, he moved among them like a bullock in ballet shoes, making sure glasses were kept filled and soon spirits were high. Jasper allowed his glass to be filled for the third time and felt a warmth flow into his belly. He kept one eye on Kate, head and shoulders above the black feathered hats, thinking what a lot of old crows the funeral had brought out. There were a few gawky younger girls alongside the women drinking tea, presumably all members of the Tremain family, but Kate seemed to shine with a quiet confidence as she moved amongst the gradually diminishing crowd.

At last Jasper managed to come face-to-face with her and offer his condolences on her loss. How crass that sounded. How bloody formal. He cursed inside.

'Mr. King!' she seemed slightly surprised to see him. 'How very kind of you to attend dear Uncle Tom's funeral. All that way, over from Tregeare.'

'It's Jasper, not Mr. King,' he smiled and watched her closely. 'It was nothing. I wanted to pay my respects, for after all we have some kind of distant family connection I believe.'

Kate's eyes met his. Had he imagined it, or had she flushed slightly to see him?

'It must be very difficult for you all here after such a shock,' he sounded genuinely concerned. 'If ever you need help of any kind, I can be at your service...'

She murmured her thanks and explained in a quiet voice that her cousin Jack would continue to run the farm, helped by his dead father's brother. She would stay on to look after her aunt, who was struggling to come to terms with her loss. She then spoke again even more quietly, so that Jasper thought afterwards as he rode homewards that he had probably imagined it. Kate said that she had started volunteering her help at the Infirmary, just one day a week. It made her feel useful she'd said with the barest of smiles, before turning back to the fragile aunt.

As Jasper rode through the leafy lanes he was glad of the time to reflect on the day's events. He did not regret the effort of attending the funeral, not for a moment. Tom Tremain now lay in his final resting place, all his strivings were over. There was a guilty moment among Jasper's thoughts when he wished his own rather pompous father was in his grave, but he quickly brushed that aside, feeling ashamed. He wished that they could get on better as father and son; he even felt an unreasonable pang of jealousy for Kate's cousin Jack, who had blubbered uncontrollably at the loss of his beloved father as he had stood at the graveside.

By the time his tired horse started to plod upwards onto Tregeare Down, Jasper was resigned to the fact that his own father thought he fell well short of what was expected in an eldest son, and a King at that. Well he'd just have to show him what he was really made of.

Then a gleam of sunlight broke through the cloud and his spirits lifted. He had accomplished one thing earlier that day, he had manipulated a brief encounter with the lovely Kate Polglaze once more. And if anything, his opinion of her had increased tenfold.

By the time he reached the lodge leading to Tregeare House, he felt in a much happier frame of mind. He could even cope with his silly, vain sister without losing his temper over dinner. He gave a gentle nudge at his horse which was already picking up pace now he was nearly home. Around the corner and the beautiful house appeared out of the dusk, candle-light shining from each window. He suddenly felt what a lucky bastard he was, for he was still very much alive, with everything to live for in this world!

A few miles down in the valley to the east, it was a very different picture. A gang of railway navvies laid down their tools for the day. Grey with dust, exhausted from a long day's graft, they washed in the cold water of a horse trough out in the open. They had been working on deep cuttings, the work made all the harder because of the hard nature of the rock. This was a very different world from that of Jasper King. These men were as tough as old boots, pale with dust, often gaunt-faced, they worked like well-oiled machines. It was a physical world, an often ugly world of predominantly young powerful labourers. They worked with picks and shovels and the work was extremely physical. But it could be dangerous work at that as they worked alongside men who were used to working with explosives. One of their workmates now lay in the Infirmary at Launceston, maimed for life.

But these men had something that Jasper King did not. They were part of a gang, a tightly-knit group of men who trusted each other in their everyday working lives.

Mostly single, they laughed together, swore at each other and even threw an occasional punch if the drink was on them. They knew they had a fearsome reputation in the local area and they relished that fact. It put a swagger in their steps and a thirst in their throats. They worked hard and they played hard. Some of them had lived really tough lives already for their age, living in temporary shanty settlements as they worked all over the south-west of England. But the money was good, much better than the pay on the farmlands, so they were all prepared to take a chance with the possibility of an accident at work. When all was said and done, it made real men of them all. No soft white hands and slack bellies for them!

The gang of younger navvies, wet hair now plastered close to their heads, walked off together with a jauntiness found at the end of a day's work. The older married men trudged towards their lodgings and their families. Railway tracks would be laid along this valley one day soon. But for now, the men were looking for a drinking spree to slake their raging thirst and their dusty throats, no matter how many of the clergy tried to warn them off public houses and the demon drink!

Chapter 11.

The Bell Inn was full to bursting. Outside the public house, the rowdy sound of men's coarse laughter could clearly be heard up and down the length of Tower Street. Old women sitting in their window seats enjoying the evening air, nervously shut their casements tight and moved back into the shadowy dusk and the relative peace of airless back rooms and sculleries. They knew, because the local newspaper told them so, that these navvies now drinking in the Bell nearby, could quite easily go 'on the rampage' before much more alcohol was poured down their necks. They also knew that these same men were poachers and thieves, again because the paper told them so and reported on their frequent fights with the local youths of Launceston town. It was no wonder the Vicar of St. Thomas urged the navvies to 'avoid public houses' warning them about the dangers to their health and wasting hard-earned money buying the demon drink, when they could all be enjoying a nice cup of tea or good coffee in the Mission Room in Priory Lane.

The noise gradually grew louder and louder, until there was a huge crash and a fight broke out, a violent melee of bodies tumbling out onto the narrow street. Drunken and wild, one of the younger navvies had picked on one of the local young men, who was himself just as drunk and disorderly if the truth was known. This was the sign for men to quickly take sides and join in the fight, so that punches were thrown haphazardly, heads received nasty blows and teeth were knocked out in what became a bloody mess! The local newspaper would no doubt report on the navvies as being 'the embodiment of evil' in the following week's edition.

Eventually the situation was calmed down by the arrival of two constables and many of those involved in the fray simply melted away into shadowy back alleys, holding sore heads and bleeding mouths. Two men lay stretched out in the street, seemingly unconscious. The landlady of the inn came out to survey the scene and, out of the kindness of her heart, sloshed a bucket of cold pump-water over both of them. Gradually their heads were lifted off the ground and they shook themselves like dogs. Groans were emitted from the beaten men, before the constables dragged them off to the dilapidated dungeon in the battlemented Southgate Arch, to cool off overnight.

The state of the prison cells was absolutely filthy and so grim that calls had gone out to close the prison down. A previous jailer had even made a request to the Mayor of the time whether the cells could be whitewashed as they were so filthy. The Mayor had supposedly replied that the blacker the prison was, the better! That it looked more like a jail if it was black and filthy. Is it any wonder that the mothers and grandmothers of the town always used to say 'It's like Launceston Gaol in here!' if their homes looked dirty or untidy in any way, without good reason. The rumour around the old place was that the Home Secretary (whoever that illustrious person might be) had issued an order that the prison at Launceston should soon be refurbished. No wonder the Southgate Arch, part of the old town wall, was known by local folk as 'The Dark House.'

So the two injured men were shocked to find themselves lying on dirty straw in the stinking cell for criminals. This was not how they had imagined their night's drinking would turn out! The local man had lost three teeth and his mouth was dark with dried blood. His left arm seemed to be useless, hanging painfully at his side. The navvy seemed slightly better off, although he was nursing a swollen black eye. Known to his work-mates as Jud, he was trying to be tough, as ever, angry that he was locked up with mere yokels, as he saw them. They were no better than animals in his view and lying on straw, as there were no beds, seemed appropriate for them. He sighed deeply. He must keep calm and wait till morning so he could then make his way back to his lodgings some four miles away at Egloskerry.

The local man, Joseph Williams who was arrested with the navvy, kept to the other side of the cell, well away from his sparring partner from the Bell. He touched his swollen mouth gently, felt the blood crusted there and explored the gap with his fingers where teeth were now missing. Perhaps the old Vicar down at St. Thomas was not quite so mad after all. Perhaps this drinking lark was truly an evil sent from the Devil himself! If he'd sat down the night before with 'a dish of tay' as his grandmother called it, instead of visiting the Bell Inn and swilling beer until he could barely stand, he wouldn't be in this stinking place with a lot of common criminals who were waiting to be taken down to Bodmin for the next Assizes.

It was a humid night, unpleasantly hot and fetid in the cell in the Southgate Arch. The stench of urine, and worse, was unbearable and sleep was hard to come by in filthy straw on the stone floor.

Across the town in the Infirmary the injured navvy was also having trouble sleeping. He lay in his pristine, snow-white bed under cool sheets, yet kindly sleep would not come to him either. He had lost all sense of time. How long had he lain here? Days? Weeks even? Often he would break into a sweat under his swaths of bandages, as blurred memories of the explosion came back to him. Flashes of bright light, pain and noise would suddenly appear in his brain and he would call out in the echoing hospital, fearful of the future. Then one day he remembered a soft, comforting hand stroking his brow and a gentle voice speaking in low tones. An angel had come to him. Well he'd assumed it was an angel for he had felt a reassuring sense of peace and well-being, but she had gone, all too soon. And now he was lying in his narrow hospital bed trying to make sense of it all.

The moon was high over the old walled town, the Norman castle silhouetted on its proud perch looking down on the jumbled roofs and narrow streets. All seemed calm now. Drinkers lay heavily snoring in bed-chambers, the old women snuffled in their dreamless sleep, children fidgeted in their cramped beds, and the Vicar of St. Thomas dreamed of the time to come when all of his flock would sit in the Mission drinking tea nicely together, avoiding the temptation of alcohol and ultimate ruin.

Chapter 12.

Peace had been restored to the streets of Launceston and the Sabbath dawned to a day of sunshine and light. Some secretly nursed sore heads but most managed to accompany families to Morning Prayer, even if they did close their eyes during the sermon and try not to snore aloud.

Back in Egloskerry, the parish church dedicated to St. Keri was packed as usual, for villagers and Penheale estate workers were still more or less obliged to attend services. Built out of so-called local 'moorstone' the church could be dark and gloomy in the short winter days, but this magnificent morning the door was open wide to let God's sunshine through the granite porch. Here Roman Catholic Mass was once conducted by a priest in Latin, but the Reformation had changed all that, many years ago. Now the people could at least understand the language in church and sing a few hearty hymns about the harvest and things they knew about!

Egloskerry church had weathered the storms of centuries and its old vicar, the Reverend Simcoe, had purchased the Penheale estate back in about 1830, or so white-haired grandfathers still told their families as they huddled around their hearths in the winter. After fathering eleven children and doing many good works, Simcoe had died in November 1868 at Penheale Manor House and was buried in the churchyard, leaving his name for posterity above the door of the local public house. Simcoe and the Simcoe Arms, was a name to be remembered among Egoskerry's parishioners and drinkers alike, which now included the navvies living at Killicoff and others scattered at Trebeath and surrounding areas.

Mary Jane Jenkin had walked with others from Badharlick to attend the service that morning after completing their daily tasks earlier. It had been a bit of a meander, as old Sarah was slowing down a lot these days, but it was such a glorious morning that the walk to church was something to be enjoyed.

There had been a lot of lively talk as they walked, and as usual the gossip came around to all the changes going on in Egloskerry village mostly due to the building of the railway along the pretty Kensey valley from Launceston.

Mary Jane was still getting over the shock of her mother's news from home, simply that her parents had somehow squeezed in eleven lodgers in every tiny nook and cranny at Killicoff, all of them engaged in working for the rail company. Then someone came up with a new bit of gossip, that some of the outlying farms at Badharlick were also going to take in navvies as lodgers.

'Well I'm damned,' old Sarah stopped and puffed heavily in the growing heat as she spoke. 'As if tedn't bad enough that they devilish navvies be all around the village causing trouble! Now us'll have to see 'em back at Badharlick too.' She shook her head in its ancient Sunday bonnet in disbelief.

'Now now Sarah,' an old, grizzled farm-worker chipped in as he mopped his weathered brow, 'Tes no good talking about being damned, tis the Sabbath after all's said and done.'

As if on cue the church appeared as they rounded the last corner, as if to remind them of the Lord's Day of Rest. Not that any of them ever seemed to get much rest, they reflected ruefully.

Bonnets and hats were adjusted, hair tidied, dust flicked off boots and Sarah's stays were tweaked into a more comfortable position, before they entered the welcoming coolness of the porch.

As Mary Jane stepped into the semi-darkness, her golden hair was lit up against the rays of sunlight coming from outside. Wisps and tendrils escaping from under her drab hat glowed, and the whole effect was like that of a brilliant halo.

The Jenkin family were seated in a neat row near the back, as always. But another figure seemed to have squeezed onto the end of the row. This person, a young man, was none other than the whistling stranger with the brightly-coloured kerchief who had seemed to wink his eye at Mary Jane, as she'd walked home on her last visit. Now he turned his face towards her and there was a flicker of recognition there too. He remembered the girl's pretty golden, copper-coloured hair, now illuminated like some angelic creature he had once seen on a stained glass window in a far-off church when he was working in Devon.

The Badharlick workers all filled up another wooden pew near the back, which was already full, with dry-rot. Apparently some architect or other from Launceston was about to write a report on the fabric of the old church, so no doubt things were about to change. But as Mary Jane looked around her, she noticed the ivy growing through the damp walls and hoped that things would not change too much. She did not like change, it made her uneasy, like the railway workers all flooding into the village to live with their strange voices and new ideas from distant towns.

She felt aware at times during the service, of being watched. She would not have turned around for the world, but she sensed that the stranger sitting with her own family kept staring at her and the back of her neck prickled. She held her head up high during the lengthy sermon and tried hard to focus on the morning prayers as she knelt on the hard wooden kneeler. Next to her was Sarah who could not kneel down any more, for if she did it would be a right old carry-on to get her up on her feet again. Instead she was bent over in the pew, her gnarled old hands clasped in prayer, probably praying for deliverance from the evils of the world about to descend on their much-loved village.

The vicar eventually reached the end of the service with a blessing to all those in the parish, and for a new sense of generosity among local people towards all those families who had recently moved into the area to work, for this was the dawning of a new age. In the momentary silence, there was a loud muttering of criticism from old Sarah in the Badharlick pew. Several heads turned around and smirked, some aged heads nodded in support, while two children sitting below the pulpit started to giggle and were quickly hushed by their mortified mother.

The congregation of people started to leave the church, relieved to get out into the cheerful sunshine, away from the smell of damp and mould. They had all confessed their sins for the week in the prayers and they could now start afresh. It would be a week of hard work for most, but they were used to it. They expected nothing more, nothing less.

Mary Jane kissed her young brothers and sisters and spoke briefly, to her parents. She could see the group from Badharlick were already starting off down the winding lane on the way back.

Hanging back behind her anxious-looking mother and her father (in a new pair of boots she noticed), was the stranger. He smiled at her winningly from behind her father's back.

She thought, like before, that there was the barest hint of a wink in his eye. She blushed slightly, turned away, and hurried past the closed doors of the Simcoe Arms to catch up with her companions.

Chapter 13.

It was the day after the Sunday service at Egloskerry and the week's work was well under way on all the farms in the surrounding district. A few miles up the lane from Badharlick, the men at Tregeare Green were sweating in the morning sunshine as they began moving the sheep from holding-pens into the barn for shearing.

William Treglown, now much recovered from most of his injuries from the attack on his way back from market, was standing in the shade under a leafy tree with his father. He was watching the men wrestling with the sheep before getting down to their back-breaking work with their shears. He was itching to help them as he usually did, but he was still not back to full strength, so he was resigned to being an observer to the familiar scene. William's mother and dear old Annie still kept a close eye on him, making sure he did not over-tax himself in the warmer weather but he hated the helpless feeling of not being of any use in the busy day-to-day ritual of work on the farm.

He turned away from the busy scene and walked slowly back to the farmhouse. It was dark and cool inside and he knew that the women would be working in the dairy, skimming cream and making junkets. Later they would be preparing food for the workers some of who were from neighbouring farms, for shearing was a task all helped each other with. There was an old local saying, 'Shear your sheep in May, and you shear them all away,' but that when it was a chilly spring and the poor animals dashed away after shearing, shivering without their warm coats. Today it was quite simply hot and no doubt the flock would be relieved to get rid of their thick fleeces.

William poured himself a drink of cold, clear water from a clay pitcher and sat down heavily on the settle. He felt it was just not right to be inside on such a day. He had seen his father ride off out of the yard to do a bit of farm business and William felt guilty to be doing nothing. He cast his mind back all those weeks to the night of the attack on him. It was those men, those strangers, who should be feeling guilty, leaving him bloody and unconscious in a ditch. But no doubt they had spent the money they had stolen from him weeks ago, and not even given him another thought!

He felt restless. He needed to go somewhere and do something. He drained the last drops of water and stood up with renewed vigour. As he passed the mirror near the window, he caught a glimpse of himself and paused. He put a hand up to his cheek where a vivid scar drew a line. It was still painful to the touch and it burned hot when he thought of the kicking he'd received, but a scar wouldn't kill him. It was just a daily reminder that one day he'd find those men and make them pay.

He saddled his beloved bay mare in the quiet stables, thinking it was only a few weeks ago that such a task would have been nigh on impossible after his injuries. He stroked her neck and she whickered with pleasure, her dark liquid eyes shining in the shadows of the stables. In the distance he could hear the muted sounds of men's shouts at the shearing and the agitated baa-ing of the flock. He led her out into the sunshine of the yard, her hoofs ringing out on the cobbled stones.

As he mounted a familiar creaky old voice shouted from the echoing dairy, 'An' where do ye' think you'm going to William? Does yer mother knaw you'm goin' out riding, all on yer own?'

Annie stood in the doorway with her hands on her ample hips, a frown on her brown wrinkled face. He could not help laughing aloud at the angry old woman.

'Oh Annie, I'm just going for a ride that's all.' He smiled at her in the disarming way he had. 'You can't keep me tied to your apron strings forever, you know.' He nudged the mare gently forward, 'and there's no need for you to be running to Mother, telling tales either. I'll not be long...' And he urged the mare into a brisk trot as they disappeared around the corner and down the lane.

A few hundred yards further on, William pulled on his reins by a granite post in the hedge, marking the parish boundary between Laneast and Eglsokerry. It was partially hidden by towering foxgloves, while vivid green ferns unfurled amidst the tangle of wild flowers, docks and nettles.

Tregeare House is just inside the parish of Laneast, but William had no desire to have a chance meeting with that spoilt Elizabeth King or even her brother Jasper come to that. He turned his mare's head towards Egloskerry and then rode away from the cluster of houses with its Methodist chapel and Post Office which made up the hamlet of Tregeare Green.

It was much hotter riding through the narrow enclosed lanes than he had imagined for the weather was dry and sultry. Before too long sweat beaded his brow and trickled down his face, and he wished he'd worn a wide-brimmed hat for protection from the sun. He cursed himself for his weakness for he was beginning to feel quite dizzy. And to think he had foolishly thought himself recovered enough to help with the shearing, back at home.

When he neared Badharlick Bridge at the bottom of the hill, he dismounted and led his horse to drink at the river. It was cool and green under the trees and he closed his eyes and slumped down in the grass, his back against the gnarled trunk of a tree. A distant rumble filled the air, suggesting a storm might be approaching.

The next thing he knew, someone was splashing refreshing water on his face. He heard blurred women's voices, as if spoken from under water.

'Tis William Treglown from up the Green,' one whispered.

'Ess, you'm right maid,' a much older woman's voice. 'The one who they awful men attacked in the darkness, back a-long.'

'Look at the scar on his face! Mind you, he's still very ansum,' said the first.

'I b'leeve you'm a bit sweet on 'un,' a snigger followed from the old woman.

'Sssh, he may hear... splash some more cold water on his face!'

William's eyes flickered and gradually opened wide. Above him were lush green leaves, barely moving in the shafts of sunlight for the air was heavy and still. The wrinkled, brown face reminded him of old Annie and he smiled drowsily at her.

'We was worried you'd passed clane out sir, down here by the river.' It was not Annie, but another old woman he vaguely recognised as being one of the ancient dairy workers from Badharlick.

Then he turned his attention to the other woman kneeling anxiously beside him. She was only a tongue-tied girl in comparison, but he was sure he knew her too. Her golden, coppery hair caught the beams of sunlight and he remembered her then, an Egloskerry girl in a flowery dress at the fete the previous summer.

He sat up, feeling a fool to have drawn attention to himself in such a way.

'I … I think I must have felt dizzy and fainted in the heat,' he said apologetically as he clambered to his feet, shaking drops of water off his shirt and picking up his riding crop. His mare was cropping the fresh grass under the trees contentedly.

'Twas a bit of luck that we were here,' the girl spoke in a quiet voice, 'we were checking the heifers in the paddock near the river. They're a bit skittish at the best of times…well just you look there!' A flash of silvery light appeared as if by magic, followed by a rumble. The young cattle suddenly seemed to go quite wild, stampeding across the paddock, flicking their tails crazily in the air.

Another flash of light and a loud peal of thunder directly over them, disorientated both animals and humans. Mary Jane clutched William's sleeve and felt immediately brazen, so she let go of her grasp as if his arm was made of red-hot metal. He gave her a quizzical, amused look. Old Sarah, unperturbed, laughed once more at seeing this. The mare, previously so tranquil, looked terrified, rolling her eyes and trembling like a reed in a wind.

William caught up the dangling reins and calmed her down, stroking her neck, speaking in a low reassuring voice. The women watched, Mary Jane quietly admiring, Sarah simply wishing she could sit down on a nearby tree stump to rest her aching back but knowing she'd find it hard to get back up.

It grew dark and strangely quiet. It felt oppressive under the canopy of the trees, but not a drop of rain fell.

William looked around at the natural beauty of the place and spoke thoughtfully, almost as if to himself, 'I believe that old Reverend Simcoe of Penheale gifted this piece of land down here at Badharlick Bridge before he died.'

The two women stared at him, wondering what on earth was coming next, for this was where they grazed cattle in these lush pastures. 'Apparently,' William's voice murmured, 'this land will be used for the new railway station which will soon be built at Egloskerry.'

A dazzling flare of lightning lit the stunned faces of the women, followed by more reverberating thunder, for the storm was about to break.

Chapter 14.

The Mayor of Launceston straightened his gold chain and cleared his throat somewhat nervously. He took out a white handkerchief and mopped his brow, for he was about to address an important meeting of the churches and the non-conformist ministers in the club room in Priory Lane, where the Mission had been formed to meet the needs of the navvies. But he knew that there was much apprehension in the district about these workers, and that the local gentry believed firmly that only the church would be their salvation.

Rows of black-suited grim-faced men sat waiting for the Mayor to begin. At the back of the room a few women in hats were putting out tea-cups and biscuits on a white cloth and whispering, for fear of incurring the wrath of the male gathering.

'These are different days here in our beloved home-town of Launceston, for the world is changing around us,' The Mayor looked over the sea of heads at the comforting text on the wall at the back of the room, 'Peace Be with You' before he continued with his theme. 'We have the railway now here in Launceston, with our wonderfully smart station with its slate and granite-built waiting rooms painted in brown and cream and lit by oil lamps. Some would say we are no longer cut off from so-called civilisation!' There was a low growl of something like approval which went around the room. He cleared his throat nervously once more and attempted a weak smile.

'The building of the railway all the way to Launceston is an enterprise which was undertaken in the face of great difficulties and many impediments.' He paused briefly, 'But the engineers and the most illustrious Isambard Kingdom Brunel did not capitulate when they encountered the many obstacles in their path. Did they give in when they saw the Tamar stretching before them? No! They rose to the challenge! They conducted surveys and accomplished clever feats of engineering to construct the Royal Albert Bridge to cross the river, to bring the railway to Cornwall so that we may now enjoy a new lease of life!'

A spattering of grudging applause went around the room before the Mayor resumed his speech, warming to his theme now.

'However the railways did not build themselves gentlemen, we must remember that.' He banged his fist on the table in front of him to drive home the point. 'So I ask you now, who built the railways?' He stared hard at the faces in the front row. 'The navvies and the sawyers, that's who! And now this honest body of men are here among us in Launceston, building the next stage of the line to Egloskerry, Tresmeer and the rest of the North Cornwall. And it is our responsibility as the townspeople to make them all welcome, some of them have their families here too of course.'

An angry voice shouted from the back, 'You call 'em honest men Your Worship, I call 'em a lot of bleddy tramps! They want nothing more than to get drunk, be rowdy in the public houses and fight our men and boys.'

'Arrh', shouted another in agreement, 'and then terrorise our daughters... and our wives on market days!' A faint cheer went up at this remark from a hen-pecked individual, who was immediately squashed.

The Vicar of St. Thomas got to his feet with his hands out in supplication. 'Peace gentlemen, we must stay calm...this will not help us. These people are here to help our community, to endure hard labour in our midst! The very least we can do as Christians is welcome these strangers to our doors. Our Lord would not have turned these people away, he would have given them food to eat and shelter for their families.' Heads nodded vehemently among the gathered clergy.

'Ess, but the Good Lord wouldn't have taken them up the hill to the Bell and bought them copious amounts of strong ale either, vicar!' The same angry voice came from the back. An outburst of laughter went around the room at the very nature of the comment, but was quickly quelled.

'These men are genuine navvies,' continued the Mayor, 'recognised all over the country for their precarious work. Some are away from their families and comforts of home for long periods of time. I believe we should start as we mean to go on, by providing them all with a tea, followed by entertainments for those with wives and children.'

At this point the applause was much louder and more enthusiastic. 'I believe the Vicar of St. Thomas would like to speak at this point,' the Mayor mopped his brow once more and sat down, thankfully.

'I believe we must urge these men to make use of this Mission Room as their own, so that they will then avoid public houses which makes them out of pocket.' He looked around mildly, 'Not all these men are hard-drinking men, but some may require a little more encouragement than others. We in the church, and the local chapels, are prepared to provide them with tea and good, strong coffee and other suitable non-alcoholic drinks here in this place.'

'What about the cost of all this carry-on? We don't give our own townspeople free tea and coffee!' A man with a red face heckled from the back. 'Tedn't right in my eyes.'

Some heads nodded in agreement with this comment, while others scowled back at the man with a face like a beetroot who persisted by saying, 'Twill only cause more trouble in the town. You'll be giving these outsiders free board and lodgings next!'

A hubbub went round the gathering and the Mayor stood up again.

'Quiet please gentlemen!' He waved his hands in a downward motion to subdue them. 'It seems the ladies are ready with the refreshments, so it's a good time to take a break.'

The chinking of cups and the appearance of vast brown teapots bore witness to the Mayor's words, soon plates of biscuits were being offered to the men as they drank their tea and talked animatedly in small groups.

'Wish 'twas something stronger than tay,' said the man with the beetroot face as he swigged noisily from the plain white china cup and grimaced.

'You didn't really think the old Vicar would be dishing out cider and ale here did you?' A man with a morose expression and no teeth replied, dipping his biscuit in his tea to soften it.

'I s'pose not... certainly as there's all these teetotal chapel folk here,' beetroot-face grimaced once again and jerked his head towards them. 'Course they're all trying to set themselves up as examples of good-living. Whiter than white they think they be!'

The Vicar moved around the groups of men, holding his teacup aloft and smiling benevolently at everyone. This was his moment of glory, not only fighting the demon drink, but helping the navvies to a better life. Fighting the Devil one might say, for a reporter in the local newspaper had only last week claimed the navvies to be 'the embodiment of evil' in their midst.

He picked up a plain biscuit thoughtfully. Launceston's elite might thank him yet.

Chapter 15.

It was hot weather and hay-making was in full swing on the farms and country estates. The older children were working out in the fields instead of sitting at their desks, so that the schoolmasters looked even more grim and bad-tempered than usual.

At Tregeare Manor, Jasper King sat astride his horse in the blazing sun watching the workers sweating as they scythed in rows. Later the sweet-smelling hay would be pitch-forked onto the carts and the women and children would follow on behind, picking up the leavings from the dry, dusty ground.

He picked up his reins and kicked his horse into a gentle walk in the intense heat. Flies buzzed noisily around the pair of them. Thank God he didn't have to work his guts out hay-harvesting on a baking-hot day like today. Life was good to him and his family, and recently he had begun to realise it more and more. If only his sister Elizabeth would appreciate it likewise. But she was too wrapped up in her spoilt world of clothes to even begin to think like that.

Jasper grimaced as he thought of her tantrums over nothing; like even yesterday she had made an enormous fuss at the table over something ridiculous, like her eggs were not perfect and exactly as she liked them! She had even shed angry tears as she ranted and raved at the poor serving girl. How he wished he could see her out in the fields hay-harvesting with the farm women in the scorching sun, then she'd see just how hard life was for some people.

He made his way back to the house, desperate for a cooling drink. As usual his mind kept wandering back to Kate Polglaze and how life was treating her at Werrington Park after her uncle's death. He would not have been at all surprised to learn that she was out in their fields helping with the hay harvest. She was a modern gutsy woman... not a feeble dressed-up doll like his sister.

As if on cue Elizabeth appeared around the corner, holding a puppy in her arms and whispering all sorts of nonsense to it. She looked up.

'Jasper! Father has said I can go into the town in the carriage if you will chaperone me.' Her pale eyelashes fluttered at her brother, who found the gesture affected and irritating. 'Please Jasper.'

He wanted to say no, just so his sister would not get her way for once. But then the long hot day stretched before him with little or nothing to do, and he wavered. Who knows, he may even catch a glimpse of Kate doing some shopping for her aunt!

When the carriage arrived with the sweating horses in Launceston, the sun was still beating down relentlessly. They passed the castle gates and above them the ancient castle stood proudly, as if guarding the old walled town. It had done so since it was built by the Normans hundreds of years ago. The Castle Green below the grim old castle keep was now a pleasant place to walk, with colourful flowering shrubs surrounding an old pump and with artistic wrought-iron seats dotted around the grounds.

Below in the valley, lay the ruins of the old Priory. Here lay piles of stones, some elaborately carved, the remains of the massive Medieval Priory that once nestled by the river Kensey. Every house, or even pig-sty, built in Launceston was said to contain stones taken from the desecrated Priory which had been wrecked and broken up on the orders of Henry VIII. And now even more desecration was taking place in the views of some people... for here the next stage of the railway line was being built, cutting through the valley. Men were toiling in the heat, their muscles aching and glistening with their sweat. Distant sounds could be heard from the valley as they worked on the hard rock just west of the railway station, the shouts of men and the harsh clank of metal hitting the unforgiving rock face.

Above them, up in the town, Jasper helped Elizabeth alight from the carriage. Ned needed to water and stable the horses which were suffering from the heat, and as usual he drove the carriage round to the back of the White Hart. What on earth the younger Kings wanted to visit the town for on such a hot day was beyond him. Still, he mused, he could get himself some ale in a hostelry to quench his thirst while they did whatever gentry folks do, which was probably not much beyond spending money!

Elizabeth disappeared into the milliner's in the square and Jasper loitered outside. He knew how long his sister took, pouring over hat-pins and feathers, ribbons and bows, so he was content to wait outside and survey the scene. Although it was not market day, the town was busy, although most people were showing signs of the intense heat, the men mopping their red faces with handkerchiefs like flags and the ladies resorting to sheltering under wide-brimmed hats and sun parasols. This made it difficult for Jasper to actually see their faces, as he searched vainly for the lovely Kate Polglaze.

He peered in through the shop window where he could see the sales assistant fussing over Elizabeth, who was sitting in an elegant chair near the polished counter piled with hat trimmings. She would be ages yet. A tinkling bell drew his attention to the open door, where two of his sister's acquaintances had just entered the shop. Jasper watched them greet each other and made the decision to leave

Elizabeth in the company of the young ladies. She would be fine and happy, he reassured himself.

As Jasper crossed the square by the butter market, he noticed a green-painted wagon with 'Werrington Park' in white bold letters on the tail-board. As luck would have it, the same drover he'd conversed with on a previous occasion, was sitting idly on top of the wagon, kicking his heels. His round puce face ran with sweat. Jasper watched with distaste as he took off his hat and ran his fingers round the inside, then flicked the sweat off with his fingers.

As Jasper approached the wagon, the drover started guiltily, and with a familiar gesture touched his forelock. What on earth did that bleddy Jasper King from Tregeare Manor want with him this time?

A few minutes later, Jasper walked away looking very satisfied with their brief, stumbling conversation. He had gleaned that Miss Polglaze of Werrington was indeed in the town that day. The rustic had been rewarded with a coin for the information, so both men were content.

Jasper mulled over the news that Kate was, apparently, visiting the Infirmary. It was where her Uncle Tom had recently passed away.

Glancing back towards the milliner's, Jasper could see no visible sign of his sister with her fringed parasol, or her fancy friends.

He made his mind up. It might be weeks, months even before he saw Kate again, so with a determined air he strode purposefully down the street in the direction of the infirmary. But as to what he would say or do when he actually got there, he had absolutely no idea!

Chapter 16.

The Infirmary was situated on Western Road, a solid-looking building of stone with tall, rounded windows behind some stout iron railings. It was the first time Jasper had been inside, for it had been recently built at considerable cost; well, so the local newspaper had stated. Living out at Tregeare, the Kings' family doctor looked after all their medical needs, which happily had not been of a serious nature so far as he could remember.

His nose reacted at the intense smell which immediately hit him as he climbed the steps and opened the double doors. A strange smell hit him, a bit like the liniment stuff the men rubbed into the horses' hooves out in the stables, but mixed with something else. Like rubber and bleach. He paused uncertain of where to go, when suddenly a nurse clad in white starched collar and apron appeared before him, like a ship in full sail.

'Yes?' She was very brusque, frowning at him from beneath thick black eyebrows. He felt suddenly extremely uncomfortable. As a King from Tregeare House he was not used to this somewhat confrontational greeting. Then he had a brilliant memory flash-back from the church service at Laneast, when the Vicar had prayed for a young man injured in an explosion while constructing the railway.

His colour deepened. 'I have come to enquire about the young man injured on the railway recently,' Jasper swallowed nervously under her unblinking gaze. This was her domain and she made it obvious she was the person in charge.

'He was working on the border of Egloskerry parish... but it may be that he was injured on our land at Tregeare.'

'Are you a relative? You can't just walk in here and expect to see him. He has received extremely serious injuries and is in some distress.' The dark eyebrows met in the middle as she frowned at him. Jasper had a momentary insane desire to laugh, for joined together the eyebrows looked like a single hairy caterpillar crawling across her forehead.

Footsteps echoed in the hallway. A doctor paused to see what was holding the nurse up. He recognised the son of Philip King from Tregeare, one of the Infirmary's benefactors be it in a small way. He was hoping to enlist more financial help from him for the mortuary very soon.

'Ah Mr. King,' he smiled and held out a hand towards Jasper. 'That will be all nurse,' he murmured in an aside, and the starched ship of a nurse sailed off down the corridor with a face like thunder.

'I hope that I can be of help to you,' the doctor quickly relinquished his somewhat clammy grasp of Jasper's hand.

A few minutes later Jasper found he was being conducted into a long room with tall windows, none of which seemed to be open. The heat was stifling, intensifying that unique smell of an Infirmary, a mixture of blood, urine and bleach. Two gaunt old men sat up in narrow beds propped against white pillows watching him, as he was led across the room.

In the corner under one of the windows, a bed was surrounded by a folding screen. What horrors were about to be revealed, Jasper had no idea, but he was already regretting his insane decision to visit the Infirmary for all the wrong reasons.

The doctor disappeared behind the screen and low voices could be heard muttering in muted tones. Jasper moved nearer the window which was too tall to look out. He wiped the sweat from his face with his handkerchief and turned to face the room. The two skeletal old men were still watching his every move.

The bed-screen moved slightly with a tiny squeak on the floorboards and the doctor reappeared.

'You can have a quick word with my patient,' he said in a low tone, 'but he is very tired. Try not to upset him... a volunteer nurse is sitting with him at the moment.' A brisk nod and he was gone.

Jasper took a deep breath and thought that he must see this through now. Blood and guts or whatever else it required him to look at. Just a quick word was all that was needed, so he pulled the screen aside and looked at the man in the sick-bed.

He saw a young man, his head swathed in bandages, lying prostrate amidst snow-white sheets. At a glimpse he also saw one arm only, draped on the bed coverlet. Sitting with her back turned towards him was the volunteer nurse, holding the one hand. She withdrew her own hand and turned to face him, and in that moment Jasper nearly fainted in the heat and the sudden shock.

Kate Polglaze, her wild dark hair hidden under a white scarf and in a white apron or uniform of sorts, smiled up at him and said in a quiet formal voice, 'Mr. King... What a surprise! I never expected to see you here.'

It seemed a long time before the silence was broken. A large old clock on the wall ticked away the seconds loudly and in a window an errant fly buzzed against the pane. Jasper stuttered a greeting in reply, having lost all his usual sense of composure and dignity. This was not what he had expected. But then, what had he really expected, walking into the Infirmary like that, on a hot day?

'Miss Polglaze. Kate…' his strangled voice did not sound like his own. He was at a loss what to say, so he said nothing more, aware of the fly's frantic buzzing in the window.

'The patient is very tired as you can imagine, but he is making steady progress,' Kate squeezed the young man's hand reassuringly as she spoke in her low, velvet-smooth voice. 'He is called Thomas Martock and he comes from the county of Dorset. As you probably know he was working on building the railway when he was caught up in an accident.'

Jasper could only watch as she gently stroked the hand of the man in the bed, stabbed suddenly by the most overwhelming feeling of jealousy. He immediately felt disgust at himself for even having such an emotion when faced with a sick man who had obviously lost an arm, and probably a damn sight more! But this was not something he had ever had to deal with before.

'She's like an angel to me,' the young man's voice had a burr to it which was not local. 'She keeps me going in this bloody awful place…' Sudden and terrible coughing overtook him and Kate helped him to sit up. She held a small metal bowl while he spat phlegm into it. Then she helped him take a sip of water.

Jasper watched in horrible fascination. He felt he could vomit. The heat and the smell of the suppurating bandaged wound from the lost arm, was over-powering.

Ten minutes later Jasper stood outside the building, propped shakily against the stone wall in the shade from the still-glaring sun. It had been an awful mistake on his part to venture into the Infirmary. What the hell had he been thinking of? He had seen Kate Polglaze, true, but a very different Kate, who made him feel strangely inadequate. He had hated every minute of the short time spent watching her ministering to that injured Martock man, feeling only an inexcusable jealousy as she comforted him and tended to his needs. Even now the only thing he could see in his mind was her small delicate hand holding, and stroking, the work-reddened hand of the navvy from Dorset.

He kicked the wall in his pent-up anger at himself, and at the world in general. He had gleaned that the navvy was definitely not injured on Tregeare land, so that at least was something his father would be pleased about. But the explosion had taken Thomas Martock's arm clean off, and the state of his eyesight remained an unknown as he was still heavily bandaged.

What must it be like to be in a dark world? To be in constant pain, and fear of what the future holds... All this human suffering, to satisfy man's desire to build a railway line which would then link Launceston to the outlying villages and towns on the North coast of Cornwall.

Jasper straightened his shoulders and walked purposefully towards the hostelries in the town square. He could not even bear to think of looking for his sister. He simply needed a strong drink... badly!

Chapter 17.

Philip King was not in a good temper. It was much too hot for one thing, and he thought of his illustrious ancestor Philip Gidley King with sympathy at the very thought of what it must have been like, living in far-off Australia in temperatures which were harsh to say the least. He had eventually been put in command of some rat-infested place called Norfolk Island, surrounded by reefs.

Apart from the heat his ancestor must have endured, he had even more sympathy with the fact that Philip Gidley King had been pushed into the Navy at the tender age of twelve by his father. Jasper's father couldn't stand the sea himself, preferring to feel the solid acres of land under his feet, land which he owned and could ride over on a decent horse. Then during the winter months he could indulge in some hunting with his wealthy cronies.

But perhaps, Philip mused, he should have been more like Gidley King who had later developed a reputation as a harsh disciplinarian, and he should have sent his own son, Jasper, off to join the Navy instead of having him at home in Tregeare Manor, getting under his feet as it were.

Looking at the sea from the Cornish cliffs or at Plymouth was quite enjoyable in Philip's view, but the mere thought of being on board a lurching ship in high seas with a lot of hairy mariners on a long voyage to somewhere like Botany Bay was the very stuff nightmares were made of!

He came back to earth. Then there was the fact that a business deal had gone somewhat awry that morning, so that it was fair to say that Philip King was in an extremely bad mood. He turned his steps towards the Little White Hart, thinking it would be best to avoid his usual friends for a while until he had calmed down.

As he turned into the doorway, he became aware of some sort of scuffle going on in the town square, so he stopped to observe. To his shock and horror he saw his daughter Elizabeth in the midst of what looked like a crowd of peasants, (he refused to refer to them as anything else). He recognised her hat with its feathers frantically quivering, as she seemed to stave off some sort of physical attack from a rather buxom woman. Elizabeth's genteel female companions stood watching on the pavement, terrified, while a small crowd jeered and shouted encouragement from the edge of the ring which had formed around the women. There was absolutely no sign of his son Jasper, who was supposed to be chaperoning Elizabeth that day.

Giving a roar which would have woken the dead, Philip King rushed into the melee, breaking the ring of onlookers. Scarlet-faced, he pushed his way through the gathering, beating people viciously to one side with his riding crop. This was his own pretty little girl, his beloved daughter Elizabeth, and he would soon save her from this bloody awful fracas!

A tussle appeared to be going on over some rather elaborate hat trimmings which Elizabeth was gripping tenaciously in her gloved hands. Her bone-white face showed an unusual determination as she struggled with the other woman, a buxom creature, who was by now getting quite breathless from trying to pull the trimmings out of her grip. But the creature managed to shriek, 'Them hat decorations are mine! Mine, do'ye hear?' She tried to wrench them once more from Elizabeth's grasp. 'I had'em put back for me under the counter at Miss Fanny's the Milliners!'

Philip King drew himself to his full height, placed himself between his daughter and her assailant and boomed, 'My good woman, you are gravely mistaken. These,' he took the trimmings out of Elizabeth's trembling hands, 'belong to my daughter, Miss Elizabeth King of the Tregeare Estate. I suggest you relinquish your grasp on her personal belongings immediately before I call the constable, who just happens to be a friend of mine.'

The crowd, no longer laughing, began to dissipate at the mere mention of the constable. No-one wanted to spend any time in dreaded Launceston Gaol. Even a solitary hour in that stinking hole was too much to contemplate!

'Did you actually pay for these hat trimmings?' Philip King's stony face was severe.

The buxom woman looked shocked. She let go of the offending materials as if they were red-hot, and shook her head in its sticky-looking straw bonnet.

'No? Well I shall have you up on a charge of theft!' Philip King's voice rose in a triumphant flourish as he sensed victory.

The flushed-faced woman looked around for her previously baying supporters, but they had scuttled off like earwigs when a stone is lifted off them. Muttering obscenities under the little breath she had left, she straightened her bonnet, tweaked her stays and attempted to walk off across the square with some sense of dignity.

Elizabeth King burst into tears, the feathers on her hat quivering once more. The shock of the past drama was just too much. Elizabeth's genteel friends surrounded her, twittering and giving comfort in the manner of the ladies they believed themselves to be.

Philip King glanced down at the rags and tatters in his hand, all that was left of the glorious hat trimmings which had given such offence. He handed them to his daughter, whose blue eyes were still spilling over with tears, prompting another outburst of crying. The ladies closed ranks around her and Philip left the comforting to their womanly ways. Sweat poured off him, for the day was still humid. And where was that bloody son of his? In his angry state of mind, it seemed all Jasper's fault. This would never have happened if his son had been looking after his sister as arranged.

As if by fate, the door of the Little White Hart swung open, only to reveal his son and heir Jasper King himself, somewhat bleary-eyed after several glasses of strong spirits, drunk much too quickly for his own good. At that very moment it may well have been better for Jasper if he had been in the Navy, sailing the seven seas and far away from his furious father, for he was innocent of the drama which had been unfolding outside the hostelry in the town square.

Philip King was bristling with ill-concealed anger as he strode up to his son who was standing on the steps attempting to read the situation outside. In a glance Jasper took in a knot of young ladies with his sister, who appeared to be snivelling in their midst. Oh hell what had happened this time, he wondered. He did not have much time to work it out before his father with a face as hard as Cornish granite stood before him blocking his path.

'I don't want another scene to amuse the yokels of Launceston town,' Philip spoke tersely to his son, who was quickly sobering up. 'I'll deal with you when we get back to Tregeare.' Jasper flinched at those words.

'I suggest you find old Ned with the carriage and take your sister home. She is in a delicate state of mind after a harrowing experience, for which I hold you entirely responsible.'

So saying, Philip King brushed past his eldest son roughly before entering the dark and deliciously cool passage-way of the Little White Hart.

Chapter 18.

The weather was still sultry, making work sticky and uncomfortable at best. At Badharlick Mary Jane had finished the early milking and Crabby had been particularly difficult, as if the oppressive morning was working on her temper too. It was enough to turn the milk sour! But the girl had too much on her mind to take much notice of a bad-tempered cow.

Since the day down at Badharlick Bridge when she and old Sarah had encountered William Treglown, she had not had a moment's peace. In her mind's eye she could see him clearly, lying in the lush grass near the river, eyes closed as if asleep. She remembered the feeling of panic that he may even be dead, that he may have had a fall from his horse or worse that he had been attacked once again. She had wanted to kiss his handsome face, to trace the line of a vivid scar on his cheek gently with her fingertips... That was before the storm broke, of course making the heifers go quite mad with fear in their paddock. It was also before William's shocking information that the piece of land down by the river had definitely been put aside as the ideal place for Egloskerry's railway station to be built.

Mary Jane and Sarah had whispered together about this awful piece of news while they had churned the butter and scalded the cream in the coolness of the dairy. It was too distressing to speak it aloud, almost as if that would make the plan happen! It was upsetting for both the women, for the paddock down by the river was such rich pasture-land and full of beautiful wild flowers and animals.

Sarah was full of scorn for the railway at the best of times, but this latest snippet was almost too much for her. She'd had a few tears and wiped them away with her voluminous apron and then her feelings turned to anger. She pummelled the butter with the wooden butter pats as if she had the directors of the railway company in her own two hands. Finally, quite worn out with her exertions, she decided that prayer was the only answer, and that her own prayers from that time on would be focussed on getting the Good Lord himself to stop the latest plans to ruin their village of Egloskerry.

Each time the two women went down to check on the heifers, they were nervous, afraid that everything may have changed. So it was inevitable that one morning they should see some men in suits, and one in a bowler hat pointing directions from a sheaf of papers, while workmen measured out the field. The heifers were on edge, clustering in the top corner of the field yet curious as to what was going on in their normally tranquil pasture.

Mary Jane had been inside Launceston Railway Station once only, and she could remember the brown and cream paint and the pungent smell of the oil lamps in the Waiting Room. It was all a bit dark, but very smart for all that, and every time the door opened there was a distinctive waft of train smoke from the huge clanking steam train sitting in the station. As she looked around the beautiful green pasture, past the young cattle huddled in the corner, she found it hard to imagine an actual railway station built here, with a station house, probably some sort of goods yard, and metal railway tracks stretching away into the distance towards Tresmeer, Delabole and other such far-off places.

She knew that a large railway cutting was being dug over at Riddon, for some of the men lodging at Killicoff with her parents were working there and they talked about it with her father. One of them, the young man who had winked at her in the lane and watched her intently in church, still made her feel distinctly uncomfortable if she visited home and he was there. It was simply the way he looked at her, as she played with her younger brothers and sisters or helped her poor mother in domestic tasks. He told her he was not working on the cuttings, but on the construction of a bridge to carry the road over the intended railway track at New Mills down the valley. One or two of the older lodgers were also working there, skilful men it seemed, grafting away for long hours at the brickwork. It seemed only too obvious to Mary Jane that, whether she liked it or not, they would be starting to build a railway station at Egloskerry before much longer.

She was always grateful to leave her old home to return to the farm at Badharlick, because things were just not the same. She hated her father's camaraderie with the navvies, the sheer cramped conditions with workmen sleeping in the old barn outside or crammed into one of the bedrooms of Killicoff. There was a strange male smell in the cottage, of stale sweat and dust and even ale. Her mother coped with the children as best she could, but the sheer influx of lodgers seemed to be taking its toll on her. She looked thin and weary, losing that little bit of sparkle that used to light up her eyes when she laughed at some small thing or other with her eldest daughter. There was not much to laugh at now. Life was simply one of drudgery.

Walking back down the lane after a visit to her family, Mary Jane pondered over it all and shook her head at the latest goings-on. The evening sun was sinking over the trees and birds were flying in flocks to their roosts. It was a scene of peace in nature and Mary Jane relished the familiar scene, wondering idly what William Treglown would be doing at Tregeare Green and whether he ever even thought of her. She smiled to herself at the thought of him and turned down the lane towards the river at Badharlick Bridge.

She passed the field where the young cattle were and her steps faltered a little as she encountered the darkness of the overhanging trees. There was rustling in the hedgerows and the sudden shriek of a young owl made her heart pound much more quickly. How silly she was being, she was letting her imagination play tricks with her. But as she continued more quickly now, on her way past the site of the station-to-be, she kept turning and looking behind her at the empty lane. She could sense something, or someone, was following her.

Faster now she walked, hurrying along with a rising feeling of panic which made her sick to the stomach. She turned up the slope towards Badharlick by the mossy old wooden signpost and her breath was coming fast now. Again she looked behind her, but the lane gleamed emptily in the moonlight. All looked at peace in the surrounding countryside.

She picked up her skirts and started to run up the steepening lane ahead. Yellow lamplight was shining in the distance from the farmhouse, which comforted her and made her think of the kitchen with its worn old settle where old Sarah was probably nodding asleep, and the dogs lying lazily on the rag rugs in front of the huge fireplace.

As she turned in at the granite gateposts, she paused to catch her breath for she had stitch from her exertions. Her breast was heaving for her breath was coming in loud gasps, yet she could not stop herself from looking one last time down the track behind her.

There in the lane, which wound like a pale ribbon in the moonlight, was the silhouette of a dark figure, which quickly ducked back into the overgrowth out of sight.

Whoever it was obviously did not want to be seen. She felt a brief feeling of panic, and a thrill of something unknown pass through her. Then she made a dash across the yard for the farmhouse and once inside, she bolted the heavy oak door securely behind her.

Chapter 19.

A few miles away from Mary Jane up at Tregeare Green, William Treglown was, in fact, dreaming of her. He was back in time, recalling the strange experience when he had slipped off his horse under the cool shade of the trees and woken to the splashing of water on his face. He remembered coming to, looking up at the green canopy of trees above him and the golden shafts of sunlight dappling the leaves. It was a peaceful feeling, just lying there on the river bank listening to the sound of the river flowing next to him. He could not really remember if he had actually fallen from his horse, but one thing was crystal clear in his mind, the face of a young woman with brilliant coppery-golden hair lit by the sunlight.

He had woken from the dream in a sweat, feeling disorientated, but quickly realised he was indeed at home in his own bedroom when his eyes focussed on the familiar embroidered text 'Love Thy Neighbour' on the wall. He knew that he was still not fully recovered from the attack on him, some months ago now, for he was prone to dizzy spells and had even experienced a couple of black-outs. But he knew better than to tell his over-protective mother, or old Annie the servant woman who adored him having looked after him since early childhood. They were like a couple of fussy old hens keeping watch over his every move as it was!

William sat up in bed and reached for the glass of water on the chest of drawers. He drank heavily until the glass was empty, then lay down and tried to settle back to sleep, but his mind was awake now and full of people and events...

The day before he had gone for a gentle ride on his beloved mare in the lanes as usual and a gleaming carriage had passed him by, which he'd easily recognised as the one from Tregeare Manor. It had been a very hot day and the old coachman Ned, who knew his father, had lifted his whip to acknowledge him. Poor Ned had looked like he was already sweating profusely up on his perch. William had glimpsed a flash of colour and feathers inside the carriage, like some exotic bird, which was the bright plumage of Elizabeth King the spoilt eldest daughter from the big house. Next to her was her long-suffering brother Jasper.

Well, William thought, he did not actually like Jasper that much either, but thought he must be long-suffering to put up with that hussy's spoilt ways. The whole parish was only too aware of Elizabeth's reputation for getting her own way where her grim-faced father, Philip King, was concerned. God help the man who eventually ended up married to her!

What on earth was he even thinking about, the idea of who might marry Elizabeth King, in the middle of the night? Perhaps it was because daft old Annie kept telling him it was time that he was a-courting? Most young men were already walking out with maids at his age, she had pointed at him meaningfully with a sticky wooden spoon as she'd said it, mixing up a lardy cake. Yes her ansum boy had been through an awful experience when he was attacked, but he was nigh on back to normal now. T'wouldn't be long before he'd be zackly again!

William couldn't help but smile at Annie's words. He'd never really been interested in girls much, apart from the odd dance or two at May-time in the village or at a Christmas gathering when girls seemed to linger under the bunch of mistletoe. He knew his mother expected something special in a future wife for her only son, her pride and joy. That weighed heavily on him. But his father never even mentioned women to him, seemingly far more interested in talking about buying a beautiful mare for their stables and which stallion would soon be covering her.

But then William's thoughts turned to the girl with the pretty hair at Badharlick Bridge once more. He remembered her voice seemed clear and sweet as she bent over him, lying there in the lush grass. She had been with an old, bent-backed woman who he'd recognised as a worker in the dairy at Badharlick Farm. Her brown wrinkled face, like an ancient prune, had reminded him of their old Annie here at home. The girl with the golden hair was an Egloskerry girl for sure, he'd glimpsed her at the village fete once in a summery dress, watching the dancing with a couple of children, perhaps a younger brother and sister.

The more he thought of her, the more he seemed to like her. She was obviously a proper country girl, for she had told him as he'd struggled to sit up in the long grass that the two women were down by the river checking on the heifers. He liked that. This was a girl who did more than think of putting silly feathers in her hat, like Elizabeth King from up the Manor. But then, he smiled, the only feathers this girl might have were ones she'd picked up by the hedgerows lost by a bedraggled pheasant... not fancy coloured plumage which had come on the railway train all the way from far-off London town.

Something else came into his mind then at the mention of the railway and it made him hot all over. Oh Lord, he had told the women that the station for Egloskerry would be built before too long down where they had found him, in the pastures at Badharlick Bridge! The horror in their eyes came back to him then, made even more dramatic because of the thunderstorm breaking all around them and the flashes of lightning. It was obvious that he had upset them both with his words, uttered carelessly at that time. William quite thought that it was common knowledge that a station would be built at Egloskerry, but perhaps the site was still an unknown on the farms. He was used to hearing all the news about the building of the railway from his father who kept an ear to the ground and was always in conversation with farmers and local landowners at the cattle markets. The railway line was slowly beginning to snake its sinuous way along through the meadows of the Kensey Valley.

He closed his eyes but all he could see were the dusty gangs of tough-looking railway navvies trudging along the lanes and across the fields. He had been told that the work was extremely physical and that many men had been maimed in accidents. He remembered one of the farm workers telling him about a young navvy who had lost an arm and possibly his sight too, who was said to be in the Infirmary at Launceston. He felt guilty then. In comparison William was not even doing any sort of work on the farm with his father, for since the accident he just did not seem to have his full strength back. He hated being a milk-sop at home, watched over by his mother. He rode out every day now to get away from it all, to have some freedom away from old Annie's excessive fussing too.

Tomorrow would be different, he decided. He would ride over to Badharlick Bridge once more and, who knows, he may even see the girl with the coppery-golden hair. There was something about the simple country girl that he liked.

He turned onto his side and settled to sleep in the darkened house.

Chapter 20.

After the happenings in the town square at Launceston when Elizabeth King had been publicly humiliated in a ridiculous fracas over some hat-trimmings, it was inevitable that there would be a fall-out between Jasper King and his father.

Philip King had returned home to Tregeare Manor late that same evening, with a face like thunder. He had been drinking copious amounts of spirits in the Little White Hart in a vain attempt to obliterate the venom he was feeling towards his eldest son, Jasper.

He hated any sort of public happening which involved the family name, which was revered locally. In fact his grandfather, Philip Gidley King, had been titled His Excellency the Governor of New South Wales for the years 1800 to 1806. In far distant Tasmania, the town of Launceston had been named in his honour after his birthplace. Now it was Philip King's heavy responsibility to ensure that nothing would damage the family name or heritage in any way – and that included the behaviour of his own offspring.

Jasper had kept a low profile at dinner that evening, making little conversation with his flustered-looking mother, brothers and sisters, eating virtually nothing of the excellent food replenishing the laden table. Elizabeth had taken to her bed after her shocking experience. He knew how angry his father would be on his return and just what a harsh disciplinarian he could be. As soon as possible Jasper had made his excuses and vacated the dining room, heading out to the stables.

The clinking of bits, stumbling hooves, breath blowing on the hay, and the warm friendly smell of the horses calmed his nerves. He stroked the neck of his favourite mare, Molly, and she whickered with pleasure. But he knew as he did so that eventually his father would demand a face-to-face meeting and he dreaded it. He hated being told what a failure he was as an elder son, but that was what he had come to expect.

Jasper sighed deeply and slapped Molly affectionately on her gleaming rump before walking towards the stable door. It was time to face his father and simply hope that he had calmed down since the embarrassing scene in Launceston square.

Philip King was standing with his back towards the empty fireplace, a goblet of his best brandy in his hand. His face was flushed with drink and he knew that he should not be having any more after the session in the Little White Hart. He looked around the elegant room, candles flickering on the table and reflected in the huge gilt-framed mirrors. Beautiful landscape paintings adorned the walls. It was a room furnished with refinement. His wife had a flair for such things. Outside the open window, the smell of cut grass on a summer evening came wafting in, with roses on its breath. He grunted and swallowed a mouthful of brandy. Life was damned good for the Kings, but what the devil was he going to do about his feckless son Jasper?

Before he had come up with an answer to his own question, the door opened and in walked his son. Jasper was a good-looking young man, tall, brown-eyed and with dark blonde hair. He had a slight trace of nerves about him, as well he should thought Philip. But at that moment something about his son's appearance reminded him of Jasper's mother in their early days, before producing a line of children, like some kind of brood mare from out of his stable.

'You wanted to speak with me father?' Jasper swallowed loudly in the quiet of the room.

Philip King put his empty goblet down on the mantelpiece, somewhat shakily. 'You're damned right I want to speak with you Jasper!' He lurched towards his son, breathing fumes of brandy over him, enough to make him keel over. He grabbed at the polished back of a dining chair to steady himself. 'That happening in Launceston this afternoon was an absolute bloody disgrace...' spittle flew out of his mouth while he spluttered, angrily '...and I hold you responsible. If you had stayed with your sister Elizabeth as you were supposed to, none of that would have occurred! That coarse woman would not have attacked her in that way... causing such a humiliating scene.' His colour deepened as he glowered at his son.

Jasper observed his father surprisingly calmly, noticing the evidence of too much drink on him. He knew Philip was not in control, but somehow Jasper did not tremble and cow down to him as usual. His father was blustering, mainly about his beloved Elizabeth and how she had been hurt and abused by the yokels of the town having a good laugh at her expense. He stood still and listened to his father's somewhat drunken ramblings, taking the criticism without flinching. But nothing seemed to placate his father, who seemed even angrier that his son was not re-acting in any way, simply standing calmly in front of him.

Philip's voice rose as he warmed to his subject. No doubt a couple of the servants would be outside the door, listening to him roar. But still Jasper stood like a statue, making no comment to rile his father even further.

'Well? What have you got to say for yourself?' Philip's reddened face was pushed up close to Jasper's own.

'Nothing father.' Jasper's voice was cool and collected.

'Nothing?' Philip snarled. 'Our family name has been besmirched today in the local market place and you have nothing to say? Where were you when you should have been looking after your sister Elizabeth? Skulking in the back room of a hostelry, no doubt!'

Jasper could not help a tiny smile creeping across the corners of his mouth. After all it was his father, not him, who was obviously feeling the effects of strong drink! The silver candlesticks on the dining table rattled as Philip lurched clumsily against it once again.

'Elizabeth was safe with friends when I left her in the milliner's father. She really did not appear to need me at all. She was surrounded by women's fripperies having a fine time with her friends and other ladies,' Jasper took a deep breath, 'and I was not skulking in a hostelry at all. I was actually visiting a badly injured young man in the Infirmary.'

Philip frowned deeply. 'What the devil are you talking about Jasper? Visiting an injured man you say? I would not consider you the sort to visit a patient in the Infirmary without an ulterior motive.'

Jasper winced as the image of Kate, her wild dark hair hidden under a pure white scarf, and wearing a pristine white apron, swam before his eyes. The truth of the barbed comment pierced his conscience. His father was not so drunk that he didn't observe this minute change in his son. 'Well? Who was this injured man?' His voice rose again. 'I presume one of our own Tregeare estate workers has been injured?'

'No, not one of ours father.' Now Jasper's voice sounded evasive, strained. 'He is one of the workers on the railway cuttings to Egloskerry, but he was severely injured... in an explosion.'

'A navvy? Is that who you visited?' Philip sounded incredulous. 'One of those good-for-nothing ruffians from God knows where, who have been drinking heavily and causing riots in all the public houses and inns hereabouts?'

'Not only the navvies drink heavily father,' Jasper muttered under his breath, foolishly thinking out loud.

A consuming flush of anger crept over Philip King's features and his son could see that he was visibly restraining himself from lashing out and hitting someone, or something.

'Get out of my sight! I cannot even bear to look at you,' Philip's voice was thick with emotion as he turned away towards the fireplace. As he heard the door being closed behind him, he swung his arm out blindly in fury at his son and at himself, sending the crystal-cut brandy goblet flying off the mantelpiece. As it landed in the stone fireplace, it smashed into hundreds of tiny slivers of sparkling glass which lay glinting in the candle-light.

Chapter 21.

The hot weather went on for days, leaving the countryside scorched and the farmworkers and the railway navvies exhausted. In that time Philip King had to go away on business, so life at Tregeare Manor seemed thankfully calmer. Elizabeth went about with an injured, melodramatic air, but got little sympathy from her brother Jasper, who avoided her company as much as possible.

Down the road a mile or two at Trgeare Green, William Treglown rode out daily, hoping to encounter Mary Jane somewhere in the lanes near Badharlick, but to no avail. Life went on and for most folk that meant hard work, with a break on Sunday to go to church and thank the Lord for all his blessings.

At Killicoff in Egloskerry, Mary Jane's mother was run ragged with her own brood of children and the sheer number of navvies lodging in their home. Sitting in the pew near the back of the church of St. Keri listening to the vicar's sermon, was the only time she ever seemed to sit down. She enjoyed the sense of peace and tranquillity for that brief time, deeply breathing in the smell of damp and musty vestments, watching the altar candles flicker in the shadowy gloom.

One Sunday morning several pews in St. Keri's church seemed emptier than usual. As the congregation filed out past the vicar into the watery sunshine after the Holy Communion service, tongues were soon wagging. It was said by those in the know that there had been more drunken scuffles the previous night in the Simcoe Arms.

'Tis the fault of them navvies, you mark my words,' croaked one of the oldest parishioners, a skeletal old fellow with considerable side-whiskers and stick-like legs.

Many gathered around in the churchyard nodded and murmured in agreement, for it seemed that nothing was ever peaceful since the navvies' arrival in Egloskerry.

Mary Jane and the Badharlick workers heard the loud discussions as they ambled past and her heart sank. After all, Mary Jane's very own family was housing the largest number of navvies in the village! Old Sarah's usually poor sense of hearing suddenly improved and she picked up on some of the words being spoken on the dramatic happenings of the night before.

'Twasn't just scuffles in the Simcoe Arms, twas a lot more'n that,' a rotund farm-worker with bright red hair from Trebeath spoke out loudly. 'My brother said 'twas more like a bloody battle!'

A few nervous looking wives tried to pull their men-folk away from the gathering, for language like that was not at all suitable for the Sabbath, especially on the hallowed ground of the churchyard.

'What I really mean is,' the Trebeath man continued in a more apologetic tone for the womenfolk, 'there was lots of blood being spilt, during the argument and the fight!'

Old Sarah, who was puffing and panting with the exertion of putting one foot heavily in front of the other, stopped dead and put in her twopennyworth.

'Tedn't right and tedn't proper fer all they ruffians to be living alongside God-fearing folk like we be, in Egloskerry!' Her voice was raised and her Sunday bonnet quivered with her pent-up anger.

Mary Jane groaned inside and tried to pull Sarah's arm to get her moving once more towards the churchyard gate. The vicar was still near the church porch talking to a small knot of parishioners, but now even he could sense that something was brewing along the churchyard path.

The vicar advanced towards the noisy gathering in the churchyard, his worn black cassock flapping in the breeze, descending on them like an old crow scattering pigeons.

The voices were becoming strident, more accusatory now, for it seemed his pastoral flock were beginning to take sides. There was even a bit of pushing and shoving going on, between those who supported the local men who were regular drinkers in the Simcoe Arms and had been allegedly attacked, and the few who supported the navvies and sawyers, mainly because they were getting good money from them for food and lodgings. Mary Jane's father was in the midst of this, getting quite vocal.

Old Sarah had just been mistakenly elbowed in her ample bosom as the argument grew more heated, and she'd sat down on the ground with an almighty thump. Mary Jane and those from Badharlick attempted to help her up amidst raised voices, while the usually gentle tones of the vicar became loud and steely as he literally shouted at them all to stop this terrible affray, in the churchyard of all places, on the Lord's Day.

The red-headed man from Trebeath slunk away down the path, keen to make his escape now that he'd had his say on the matter. So too did the ancient, whiskered man with legs like sticks. The flustered wives and their men-folk, including the Jenkin family, quickly followed suit. Only Mary Jane and the Badharlick group were left, as they struggled to help Sarah up onto her legs. She was a hefty woman and this was no mean feat, but eventually they succeeded and Sarah was none the worse for her ordeal, although somewhat dishevelled-looking, with her bonnet sadly squashed.

'Now let that be an end to it,' the vicar's voice had resumed its gentle tones. Secretly he was keen to get back to the Vicarage and the mutton pie which his housekeeper had promised. All this bother about fights in the Simcoe Arms and bad-feeling towards the navvies was something he could well do without. When the last stragglers had wound their way through the churchyard gate, he disappeared back into the church to check that the candles had all been blown out and to pick up his hat and prayer-books.

'Lord, they know not what they do,' he spoke softly to the silence.

'Who could have believed that the coming of the railway could cause so much bad feeling in a quiet Cornish parish like ours,' he sighed aloud, as he closed the heavy church door behind him.

Chapter 22.

The doors of the Simcoe Arms were tightly shut as the vicar in faded black cassock passed quickly by on his way back to his waiting mutton pie at the vicarage. The inn did not open on a Sunday and no signs were to be seen of the drama of the night before. But if he had looked really closely, he may have seen evidence of spots of rust-coloured blood on the paint of the window sill.

Things settled down for a few days in the village, although many men (both navvies and locals) could be seen sporting purple bruises around their eyes and more than a few split lips, which had been bloodied in the affray. Folk were very wary of commenting on these injuries, except for the small knot of women who gathered for a gossip in the Post Office under the pretence of buying stamps, or a pinch of seasoning for a family meal. The women feasted on the scraps of information which had been dealt out in very small parcels by their tight-lipped menfolk.

At Killicoff, Mary Jane's mother wore a martyred expression and tried hard to ignore the fact that at least four of her lodgers bore the scars of having been involved in the fight at the public house. Her husband was bad-tempered and kept a low profile, spending any free time in the evenings working in the vegetable patch behind the cottage. But it was the Jenkin children who suffered many abusive comments in the playground at school in the following week, as the village children regurgitated conversations about 'those trouble-making navvies' that they'd overheard in their own homes.

Life at Badharlick for Mary Jane was much the same. Work was long and hard, the uncomfortably hot days seemed to be coming to an end, and old Sarah was still muttering under her breath about 'they ruffians' meaning the navvies, and the indignity she had suffered in the churchyard being physically knocked to the ground after the Sunday service.

One morning Mary Jane walked off down the lane to check on the heifers in the lower pastures by the river. Sarah had remained in the dairy, mumbling to herself and puffing heavily as she churned the butter. It was a beautiful morning, not as hot and heavy as it had been, and Mary Jane relished the bird-song and the brief sense of freedom away from the confines of the farmhouse and yard.

As she reached the bottom of the lane where three roads met, she could hear the sound of a horse clip-clopping down towards the ford. She quickly crossed towards the river and the shelter of the overhanging trees, but not before the horse and rider appeared around the bend and started to wade easily through the ford, where the river-level was very low due to the recent hot weather.

William Treglown pulled on the reins and let his mare stop to drink from the cool water. As he looked up, he glimpsed a movement under the trees and recognised the coppery-golden hair that had been so much in his thoughts recently.

'It's the golden-haired girl,' he spoke to himself in a low murmur, 'the girl from Badharlick.'

He pulled his mare's head up, much to her annoyance, and they waded across the ford and up onto the lane near the trees.

Mary Jane was hiding behind a gnarled oak tree, for she knew it was William and had 'come over all unnecessary' as old Sarah put it. Her heart was hammering away, for she had not seen him since the day of the thunderstorm.

She saw the bay mare move into sight, reins dangling, rider-less. At that moment, a man's voice spoke from the other side of the tree.

'I know you're there, you may as well come out of hiding.'

She flushed. 'I'm not hiding... well, not really.'

William's handsome face with its distinctive scar appeared around the tree trunk, smiling.

'I'm on my way to check on the heifers,' her voice faltered. 'Like last time, when we found you here, lying in the grass. Before the storm broke and they went quite crazy.'

'I've been looking out for you, to say thank you for looking after me when I fainted and fell from my horse.'

Mary Jane flushed and twisted her apron in embarrassment. 'Twasn't nothing... Sarah and I were just worried that you'd hurt yourself when you passed out under the trees. So we splashed cold river-water on you to bring you to your senses.'

'Well there's not much water running in the river today,' William said ruefully. 'But it is very pretty down here,' and he smiled at her again, for he was not simply referring to the surroundings. He was amazed at his own confidence when coming face to face with the girl he'd been thinking of on those long hot nights when he could not sleep.

'I think I owe you an apology,' his voice was low. 'I blurted out about the land here being gifted by old Simcoe of Penheale, and how the new Egloskerry railway station will be built here quite soon. It was quite obvious to me that you were both upset by the news.'

He looked at her then, took in the coppery-golden hair glinting in the rays of sunlight filtering through the rustling, dry leaves above them and her sorrowful expression which said it all.

'I truly thought you would have known about it, you see,' his eyes were pleading with her.

She nodded almost imperceptibly. ''Twas a shock to us both!' She sighed. 'Old Sarah who was with me, hates anything to do with the railway and its coming. She says it seems to bring nothing but bad luck to the village... folk keep fighting and falling out.'

'But it's all in the name of progress, well so my father keeps telling me,' he smiled wryly at her.

She fidgeted a bit, at a loss. Then, 'I really must go sir, I shouldn't be here talking when there's animals to be looking at... and then there's so much to do in the dairy back at Badharlick. I've left poor Sarah churning the butter.' She turned as if to leave.

'Please don't call me sir,' he took hold of her arm to stop her. Her skin was wonderfully warm and smooth. His voice was softer. 'I'm simply William Treglown from a farm at Tregeare Green. I'm not the glorious Jasper King from the Manor you know.'

Their faces were quite close now. He could see her simple beauty, wide clear eyes with hazel lights in them, and her face framed by the amazing coppery-golden hair.

She blushed. 'And I am Mary Jane Jenkin, from Killicoff, a small-holding on the Penheale estate.'

She pulled her arm away gently. 'And now I really do have to go to the lower pasture to see the heifers... William.' She could feel his fingers on her arm still.

He watched her go, his heart singing like the birds around him. He would see her again before too much time passed. That he knew.

He collected the dangling reins of his mare and led her out of the semi-darkness of the trees into the light.

Soon the staccato hooves could be heard trotting back up the hill in the direction of Tregeare Green.

Chapter 23.

When the news reached Launceston about the scuffle at the Simcoe Arms involving locals and those building the railway, people re-acted in different ways. The editor of the local newspaper relished it and wrote a highly coloured, exaggerated piece in which the Simcoe Arms sounded like an absolute den of iniquity and its customers were all drunken sots. He was wildly excited to be able to report on something other than the morbid deaths of aged Launcestonians, or ladies in hats serving chapel teas. The vicar of St. Thomas nodded knowingly, and so doing allowed his soaked biscuit to drop into his tea-cup. It was all down to the demon drink as far as he was concerned.

In the town itself, the many inns continued to do good trade. The weather was changing, cooling down now as summer ended, but a glass or two of ale was always welcome after a day's hard graft whether you had to drink next to a navvy and his mates or not.

In the Infirmary there were more casualties, especially among those men working on the Red Down cutting near the approaches to Egloskerry. The work there was harder than most and navvies were often injured. But so far no-one had been fatally injured and the most serious incident remained that of Thomas Martock, the poor young man who had lost an arm and whose eyes were still covered in heavy bandages. His so-called 'Angel', Kate Polglaze, still tended him with sympathy and calm understanding. She could see only too clearly what the men building the railway had to endure.

His Worship the Mayor sat in his chamber reading the Launceston Weekly News, hoping that this frequent fighting between local men and navvies would calm down with the oncoming winter. The hot summer seemed to have heated up the tempers and spirits of all and sundry leading to violence and mayhem, and now it had even reached the peaceful village of Egloskerry some four miles off.

Then came much gossip that some of the work on the building of the railway line was being delayed as one or two local landowners were holding out for more compensation. Wrangles were taking place even at this late stage between lawyers for the families with the much-needed land, and the railway company. In the White Hart on market day, several landowners could be seen with their grizzled heads together talking long and hard. Occasionally the words 'compulsory purchase' could be heard, spat out with considerable venom. This, it seemed, would be the next step if agreement could not be reached.

Jasper King entered the town's best hotel and glanced around swiftly to see if his father was there with his well-to-do cronies. Finding no signs of Philip King anywhere he immediately relaxed, ordered a glass of the best local ale and took a good, long drink. He had escaped from the chore of having to accompany his sister Elizabeth that day, for she was still in the mind that the townspeople would all be laughing at her, due to her recent humiliating experience in the square.

Launceston was extremely busy as it was market day, and Jasper could see many weathered country faces that he knew well and he nodded in friendly acknowledgement when he was addressed. He noticed a small group of men talking animatedly at a long table in the corner, and recognised them as local farmers and landowners from along the Kensey Valley.

A wry smile crossed his handsome features. He knew what was going on at that table! As usual the building of the railway line, as it slowly snaked its sinuous way out of Launceston, was causing much heartache and trouble. But could he blame the men who were clearly wrangling over the required use of their land, their dearest and most valuable possession? Their acreage had probably been passed down from generation to generation. Their cattle and sheep had grazed on it down the years, in the lush and peaceful valley. And now they had to face the fact that metal railway tracks and a monstrous iron horse would clank and hiss its way across their fields, whether they liked it or not! Could he really blame them for demanding more money than they had been offered so far?

A tap on his shoulder made him turn around too quickly, slopping his ale on the floor. Thankfully it was not his father facing him, with whom he was still on a difficult and strained footing. A smiling, ruddy face greeted him, that of a friend named Isaac Penhale. He farmed out on the edge of the moor and lived with his family in a dilapidated run-down manor near St. Clether which had seen better days.

There followed much back-slapping and hand-shaking, for the two had not seen each other for some time. Jasper liked Isaac immensely, despite their differing backgrounds. The Penhales were faded gentry, struggling now with debt and a crumbling family seat which dated back hundreds of years. Jasper's situation was in great contrast, living in the stunningly refurbished Tregeare Manor in new wealth and opulence. However the two of them had forged a bond when young boys at the local school in Newport 'for gentlemen's sons' and they still got on 'like a house on fire' to quote Isaac's sweet-natured mother, who was fast becoming as faded as her once-glorious home.

Jasper drank the last few drops of ale and ordered a bottle of the White Hart's best claret (for he felt his friend looked in need of sustenance and support, judging from the worn state of his coat), and they adjourned to a quieter corner of the room.

The wine flowed and their tongues were loosened, as they caught up with each other's news, mostly depressing from Isaac's side of the table. They'd had to sell off some of their land to pay off pressing debts and the roof of the ancient house was leaking buckets in the recent thunderstorms. Then there was his father who was unwell, and his mother who was as thin as a rake... Isaac took a comforting gulp of wine and shook his head. His mother had been pressing him to find a nice young girl to marry, preferably someone with some money, who would help them out of their difficulties.

'Which 'nice young girl' would want to get tied up to a penniless idiot like me?' Isaac said mournfully as he fiddled with the stem of his empty wine glass.

Jasper poured the dregs of the bottle of wine into Isaac's glass and sympathised, 'You may have a few problems with money, but you're certainly not an idiot Isaac. Don't let anyone tell you so.' He stood up to get more wine and lurched against the table. 'I think perhaps we should have something to eat with the next bottle.'

'What about you then?' Isaac asked, when Jasper returned after ordering more wine and plates of roast beef.

'Oh, I'm having the same old arguments with my father, and frequent fallings out with my silly sister Elizabeth.' Jasper pulled a face. 'Mother wants me to meet someone, like yours does, so once in a while they introduce me to the most dreadful girls with what father calls 'a pedigree' meaning they're from good family stock.' He stopped and smiled suddenly at a thought, 'It all sounds like the annual agricultural show, showing the best cows and calves for miles around!'

Isaac let out a bellow of laughter and Jasper joined in. But the image of Kate Polglaze suddenly appeared out of nowhere in his mind and he stopped abruptly.

'Actually I have met someone I like.' Jasper's voice became quieter and his look serious.

Isaac leaned across the table towards him, 'Well come on then, tell me all.' He paused, 'I suppose your father does not approve of this girl, or you would be looking much happier.'

'Father does not even know she exists.' He paused, 'I am not even sure that she knows that I exist when all is said and done...' his voice tailed off.

During the next few minutes the two talked intimately, Jasper telling all there was to say about the beautiful and kindly Kate who was still staying with her frail aunt at the Werrington estate. How she came from a family with little money 'down West somewhere'. He knew that someone like lowly Kate Polglaze would not meet the approval of his grim-faced father. But he quite simply could not get her out of his mind.

Isaac listened quietly without interrupting, nodding in agreement at the ludicrous idea that the proud Philip King could ever give his blessing to Jasper getting tangled up with a young woman with no breeding and no background.

'Tell her how you feel about her,' Isaac urged despite the misgivings in his mind. 'After all, you've got nothing to lose. My dear mother always says, 'Love will find a way'... and she has not given up on my own dire situation yet.' He looked around at the busy, noisy room. 'Who knows? Even now a pretty girl with pots of money may be about to walk into this very room and fall into my arms!' He laughed mirthlessly and Jasper smiled ruefully across the table at him, before sloshing more red wine into their empty glasses.

A big-breasted serving-girl with a flushed face and bright eyes appeared suddenly at their table carrying huge plates of roast beef. She placed them down carefully on the wine-stained tablecloth, leaning over Isaac and revealing an ample cleavage of creamy flesh. Isaac averted his eyes and grinned across at Jasper. As she walked away from their table, looking back over her shoulder flirtatiously at Isaac and swinging her ample hips in a most provocative manner, an outburst of friendly laughter followed her back to the kitchens.

Chapter 24.

The weeks passed and the weather became autumnal, with chilly mornings and the valleys wreathed in mists. Bright, crisp afternoons were relished by those working outside on the farms and those grafting on the construction of the railway line. Leaves fell in their thousands, spinning down in reds, yellows and copper like so many coins, littering the ground. Old men and boys employed on the country estates raked the leaves into piles and soon the smell of smoking bonfires challenged the senses. The harvest had long been gathered into the barns and Harvest Festival celebrated in the churches and chapels by all the parishes.

In the village of Egloskerry there were no more scuffles in the Simcoe Arms and the vicar could eat his cold mutton pies in peace. At Badharlick, Mary Jane and the others worked hard as usual on the farm and in the dairy, yet she still managed to meet William on rare occasions. The lush pastures down by the bridge where the heifers had once grazed, had been cleared in readiness for the building of the new railway station. At Killicoff the Jenkins family struggled to feed and maintain their lodgers, who were a motley bunch of tough men when all was said and done.

Mary Jane visited her mother when she was able to lend a hand, but it did not feel like her childhood home any more. Now it reeked of male sweat and tobacco, like some kind of back-street inn. Not that she had any experience of such a place! Just walking past the open doors of the Simcoe Arms was enough for her, the smell of the smoke and of stale beer made her wrinkle up her nose in disgust. The loud voices in strange accents coming through the doors seemed threatening somehow and she hurried down the lane back to the farm at Badharlick like the Devil himself was chasing her.

On one bright October day she had seen William riding down the hill from Tregeare, his mare slip-sliding on her smooth metal shoes. Mary Jane had paused by the yard gateway to talk with him, quickly looking back over her shoulder to check that no-one was watching her when she should have working hard scouring milk pans in the dairy. They had become more confident when talking with each other since the incident under the trees earlier that summer, and she loved his gentle-ness, a quality she rarely saw in the men she worked with on the farm. They were all crude talk and bluster. William was warm-hearted and sensitive. But he knew that he had not been the same person since the violent attack on him many months beforehand. Deep inside, he was still harbouring a steely determination to get even with those who had robbed him and left him for dead in the ditch at Athill.

The young couple felt the growing pull towards each other more and more, but Mary Jane knew well that William was a class above her in the way of things. She was only a country girl 'in service' on a farm, while he was an only son and much beloved by his mother, Joan Treglown, who thought she had 'breeding' if all the local gossip was true. It seemed obvious to Mary Jane that Mrs. Treglown would set her sights on someone from a better class for her William, when his future and marriage was being planned.

As for William himself, he took pleasure in his developing friendship with Mary Jane. He had a hazy idea that in the dim and distant future the two of them would be 'a proper couple' and he imagined Mary Jane with her coppery-golden hair working alongside him on their own acres at Tregeare Green.

Towards the middle of the month, Mary Jane had a few precious hours off and she left Badharlick to visit her mother and family at Killicoff. The walk did her good in the mellow sunshine, the crisp leaves scattering underfoot and into ditches and gulleys. Across the valley she could hear the distant sounds of men's echoing shouts and the metallic ring of spades and picks on hard rock. The railway navvies were hard at work.

She clutched her basket tightly with its new-laid eggs, and increased her pace towards pretty Penheale Lodge and Killicoff opposite. When she approached she could see the newly-painted trap outside of her great-uncle Prout, her mother's uncle. Father always said he gave himself too many airs and graces, but put up with him for his wife's sake, probably in the vain hope that some of Uncle's money might one day come their way in his Last Will and Testament.

As she pushed open the door, Mary Jane could hear Uncle's deep voice and her mother's twittering, bird-like replies. She paused, listening in the porch, Uncle was talking about a terrible event that had happened some fifty years beforehand, a murder out on the moors near Roughtor.

'A milkmaid she were, worked for that Peter family out at Penhale Farm, at Tremail,' Uncle John shook his grizzled head. She were an ansum maid by all accounts, but she liked talking to the young men thereabouts, well so my father used to say. But her pretty face dedn't do her much good, for she were found dead out by Roughtor ford on the moors with her throat savagely cut...'

Mary Jane took a step into the room and Uncle's jaw shut up like a trap. He was sitting on the worn old settle by the fire, his gnarled hand holding his clay pipe, while Mary Jane's mother stood at the scrubbed table surrounded by a conglomeration of bowls and cooking utensils. Her tired face lit up to see her daughter, who kissed her mother, cleared a space and deposited the basket of eggs on the table. 'Mary Jane! What a surprise! Come in and sit down my dear. As you can see, Uncle has come to visit us from Tremaine.'

Mary Jane perched on a chair the other side of the fireplace and Uncle John nodded kindly at her, then stuck his pipe back in his mouth and puffed away contentedly.

There was a wonderful, homely smell of bread baking in the room so that Mary Jane could almost imagine it was like the old days, before her parents had taken in railway navvies as lodgers.

'Where are the younger children Mother?' Mary Jane looked around for her little brother and sister, for it was unusually quiet.

'Oh I sent them out to play up in the orchard when Uncle arrived. I'm sure he doesn't want children chittering away when he's come to visit us at Killicoff!' She smiled benevolently at Uncle and continued to vigorously stir a mixture in a huge glazed bowl. 'Tes a lovely day and the fresh air will do them good.'

Mary Jane visualised the little 'uns playing in the orchard, running wild, climbing trees and getting up to all kinds of mischief.

'I heard you telling a tale when I came in Uncle,' Mary Jane untied her shawl and smoothed her wayward hair.

The Uncle took his pipe out and looked across at her with a serious expression. 'Twas a true story, from off the moors. It happened some years ago when I were nort but a young boy, about a lovely maid, Charlotte Dymond, who met her end at Roughtor. Twas a tragic tale, Mary Jane. But too gruesome to tell an innocent young maid like you!' He stuck his pipe back in his mouth and puffed hard, a small cloud of blue smoke billowed across the hearth.

'But one thing you can learn from it our Mary Jane, is to be wary of young men who say one thing and mean another!' Uncle tweaked his beard and stared at her hard.

It was almost as though he could see her talking and smiling with William Treglown. But one thing she knew for sure, that her sweet William would not harm a hair of her head!

Some hours later, Mary Jane walked back to the farm at Badharlick. The evenings were drawing in now, there was a chill in the air and the moon rose over the valley as she thought back over the events of the day. She thought of the tragic milkmaid Charlotte Dymond who had been murdered in a lonely place out on Bodmin Moor, and every little sound, every rustle in the hedge frightened her. She kept looking behind her along the moonlit lane, thinking of the man who had followed her that time ducking into the dark cover of the undergrowth.

She had never been so glad to see old Sarah's familiar face at the kitchen window, lighting the oil lamp, when she reached the farmstead at Badharlick.

Chapter 25

As the autumn changed the landscape into bright colours and carpets of leaves, the work on the railway line continued but progress was slow. The land had all been purchased, in some cases by compulsory purchase where owners had refused to accept the compensation deals offered by the railway companies. The talk was, even more navvies were being drafted into the area to make up for the lost time spent in wrangling, so lodging houses had to be made available for the incomers.

The people of the surrounding area had grown used to the sight of fearsome-looking, muscular men, who spoke in strange dialects working in their midst. But that did not mean they liked it! There were still those who thought the navvies were drunkards and wastrels, despite the long, hard hours of graft they put in every working day.

At Egloskerry, men in top hats from the railway company could be seen with maps and charts at the site where the new railway station was to be built. The halcyon days of the heifers peacefully grazing that pasture-land were gone for ever... Mary Jane would walk past, on her way to church or to Killicoff, her eyes averted. Life was changing rapidly and she could not come to terms with it all. At times William would try to explain gently how it was all in the name of progress, but she would shake her head and sudden tears would appear in her tawny eyes.

Then November came and with it heavy rain. This held up work on the railway line and often there were problems with cuttings being made which caused land-slides. Loosely bound earth became saturated and liable to collapse, so that the navvies returned from their days at work sodden and covered with mud and filth. Once they had sluiced the worst of it off, the younger navvies made their way to the warmth and solace of the local public houses in Launceston and the villages.

'And who can blame them when it comes down to it?' the Mayor of Launceston commented to his wife, in the comfort of their parlour, toasting his toes in front of a glowing fire.

His wife sniffed her disapproval, shook her head, then continued with her fancy needlework by the light of the lamp.

'Well they're just young men and boys, living far from home, needing a bit of company,' the Mayor was not convincing his lady-wife by any means, but he continued, 'As long as there's no more fighting or trouble, we must bear with it!'

He took a cigar from an ornate box on the side-table next to him and lit it from the fire with a taper.

'I think I'll have a word with the Vicar of St. Thomas,' he said thoughtfully as he stood in front of the fire-place, warming his backside and drawing on his cigar. 'Perhaps the Mission down in Priory Lane could provide one of their splendid teas for the navvies and those with wives and children.' He paused, 'Some of those look like pathetic little waifs and strays.'

In an acid voice his wife cut in, 'The dear Vicar will be only too pleased I'm sure. He is willing to try anything to keep these dreadful men away from the demon drink!' Then she jabbed her needle viciously into her tapestry, as if it was actually one of those troublesome navvies, so much talked about in the ladies' circle.

Just down the road from the Mayor's home was the Infirmary. It had been busier recently, now that the weather had changed and more working men were being injured in the terrible wet conditions.

The young navvy, Thomas Martock, who had lost an arm some months earlier in an explosion, was still lying in a hospital bed listlessly; but there was said to be hope that he would regain some, but not all, of his sight. The bandages had been taken off his ugly head wound, but his eyes were still lightly bandaged over. He was getting used to the frightening fact that he had lost an arm, but an unexpected visit from his worn-out mother from afar, who had done nothing but weep copiously at his bed-side for her poor, helpless son, had set him back on his road to recovery. In his tortured mind, Kate Polglaze was still 'his Angel', as she quietly went about her duties as a volunteer nurse. She gave him strength in the simple, calm way she spoke to him, encouraging him to be strong. There would be a life for him after all this pain and suffering. But God knows what sort of a bloody life it would be, he thought to himself, at least a hundred times a day.

As for Kate herself, the past weeks had been busy, both at the Infirmary and at Werrington, living with her Aunt Nell and cousin Jack. She was often exhausted, returning from hours of bandaging stinking wounds and emptying pots of urine. But wasn't this what she had wanted to do? To be useful, and help others not so fortunate? Her Aunt Nell was a shadow of her former self now that her husband was dead, talking to herself through the long hours and pottering to and fro in the kitchen at the farm in Werrington. Kate spent time trying to help her aunt, but she had retired seemingly into another world, a past time of people who were dead and gone.

At times Jasper King would flit into Kate's thoughts. Then she would think back to their unexpected meeting at the Infirmary. She wondered what had gone through his mind, seeing her in her volunteer nurses's uniform, her hair hidden under a white scarf looking like some kind of nun! He had looked shocked that was certainly true, but she remembered too the way he had stared at her own white hand holding the bruised and battered hand of the patient, Thomas Martock, before she had quickly withdrawn it. Had that been something like a glint of jealousy in Jasper's eyes? She was aware of some feeling between them, something she could not define yet. There was something about him she liked, although their first meeting that market day and during lunch at the White Hart had been marred by the spoilt behaviour of Elizabeth, his sister. Even now it made Kate smile to herself, just to think of her parting shot to Elizabeth from the Werrington Park trap, 'You should be used to the smell of cows' shit, living out in the country!' She also clearly remembered Jasper's look, not one of disgust, but of total admiration.

Well, she sighed, no doubt she would see him again before too long. Perhaps at the market on a Tuesday, for she often went there on errands for her aunt who rarely left home these days .

So the days passed in the cold, wet month of November: The roads were awash, Launceston town square was full of puddles and filth after the cattle markets, and, almost a mile or so of railway track was painstakingly laid down in the Kensey Valley.

Then something happened which everyone in the area had dreaded, but half-expected. There was a landfall of earth and rock at the infamous Red Down cutting near the approaches to Egloskerry.

There were several casualties and some were taken to the Infirmary at Launceston in horse-drawn carts to have their injuries treated. Others were in a state of shock, neither speaking nor moving from the scene of devastation, standing like statues of mud in the pouring rain. But worse by far, one man who had just finished his shift in the torrential rain, was killed from the falling material.

His navvy work-mates refused to leave him. They dug him out of the sodden earth with their spades and their bare hands.

Chapter 26.

A mood of grey gloom had descended over the Cornish market town of Launceston. The relentless November rain sluiced down upon the ancient castle and the fields in the valley below were flooded. The work on the railway cutting at Red Down, or Riddon, had halted temporarily, after the tragedy. The dead man was said to be named Edward Harvey, known as Eddie to his stunned work-mates.

In the tap room at the White Horse Inn, a few old men sat in the tall settles, near the fire. They were drinking the local cider and mulling over the recent terrible tragedy, describing it with some relish it may be added.

'Twas an awful sight be all accounts,' a thin man with a mournful face and a single tooth in his mouth sighed, before swilling back some more scrumpy. 'They navvies worked like slaves to dig that there man out o' the mire.'

'Who was it told 'ee bout it then?' enquired an even thinner man, with an emaciated face the colour of lard.

'Will Smale out 'Skerry told me. He were there at the time! Niver seed anything like it, 'ee said.' He paused for dramatic effect and the old men leaned forward, not wanting to miss one word. 'The rain was teeming down, there were strong, grown men on their hands and knees scrabbling in the mud, an' some of they younger boys working out there with the horses were crying like babbies!' He sucked his remaining tooth and shook his head sadly.

'Don't'ee stop there, Jack,' an earnest-looking man with an old-fashioned felt wideawake hat leaned even further over towards him.

Jack drained the dregs of his cider and put the empty mug down with meaning on the small wooden table covered in rings and marks from years of past drinking.

'I'll get 'ee another jar o' scrumpy Jack, but don't 'ee tell yer tale till I'm there listening mind!' The man with the wideawake hat hurried to the bar and banged the empty mug on it loudly.

Mug filled to the brim with strong cider, Jack continued his sorry tale, preening somewhat at being the centre of attention for once in his humdrum life.

'Twas like this,' Jack took a noisy swig of his scrumpy, enjoying the moment as the old men leaned even further in towards him, 'After some digging an' scrabbling about like crabs in the mud, one of they navvies shouted out that he'd found something.' He paused again, even more dramatically, looking round at the wizened old faces and watery eyes. 'Twas a hand, sticking up through the filth which was oozing all around them.'

A sound like an 'ooh' or 'aar' seemed to come from his captive audience, with much shaking of ancient heads.

'They navvies started tearing at the mud like they was mad men, Will Smale said. Diggin' all round this 'ere hand, till they cleared a patch fer his face, so as he could breath again.'

'And did ee?' the lard-faced man asked, huskily.

Jack looked at him with unveiled contempt. 'Course he didn't. Poor chap were as dead as a doornail! Well, ee'd been buried alive... But the look on his face was enough to scare his workmates witless, be all accounts.'

The old men shuddered and were silent. They had absorbed the tale, their minds full of the horror of it all. The very thought of being buried alive was too much of a terror to begin to imagine.

They sat supping their rough cider, immersed in their own thoughts.

A burning log fell onto the hearth, the sound making the old boys jump as they were deep in their own imaginings. The man with a face the colour of lard, picked up the heavy poker and pushed it back out of harm's way. He groaned with the effort as he stood back up.

"Tedn't the only tragedy hereabouts with building this bleddy old railway line,' a new voice broke in to the circle of cider-drinkers.

They all looked up, Jack some vexed that his re-telling of the latest drama in Lanson had not lasted longer to give him another free drink at the very least!

A younger man, a stranger, had come in quietly and was sitting slightly behind the settles near the window. He had listened to Jack's tale, unseen.

The old men swivelled to look at him, and he came and stood near the dying fire.

' Twas only a couple of years ago that there was a terrible haccident out to Tower Hill, only a few miles from here,' the stranger said. 'Do'ee remember it?'

The old men searched their fading memories, some seemed to have an inkling as to what he was referring, a tragedy which had been reported in the local newspaper. Others shook their heads.

'A young boy got his foot caught between the rails... He were trapped see.' They all tried to picture this terrible scene. The stranger dropped his voice before he continued, 'Then the wheels of a heavy wagon passed over him. Killed the poor boy outright it did.'

This story also made grim listening. The old men's silence afterwards was deafening. The only sound was the crackling of the fire as the stranger threw on some bone-dry sticks from a nearby basket, to catch alight on the glowing embers.

The moment was broken by the landlord's plump wife bustling in noisily with some pewter tankards. Her smiling face froze as she saw the miserable gathering of silent old men clustered by her fireside.

She banged the tankards down deliberately on the bar with a loud crash and all the old men, who were miles away, jumped near out of their scrawny skins.

'Tis like the Town Mortuary in 'ere,' she scolded. 'What iver's going on? You'll be drivin' my customers away! You've all got faces like fiddles!'

The man with the mournful face, Jack, who had been regaling them earlier with the story of the recent accident at Red Down, looked up at her from his seat on the settle. 'Aar well 'tis like this maid. We'm your customers, like it or not,' he preened momentarily, 'and 'tis difficult to look all smiley and happy when we'm talking about the terrible doings round 'ere.'

'What terrible doings?' The landlord's wife tried to look less jolly, which was difficult for her as her round face (atop of several chins it must be added) was normally wreathed in smiles.

The man with the lard-coloured countenance attempted to clear his throat and then spoke in his usual husky voice, 'We've been talking bout the railway cutting accident out at Skerry Missus. That poor man, who was killed at Riddon t'other day.'

The landlady's face assumed the respectful look of one talking about the dead. 'I've heerd tell that he's to be buried in the churchyard over by the river, at St. Thomas.' She picked up a tankard and polished it unnecessarily with a clean cloth, suddenly wanting to be busy.

'Tes true,' Jack nodded his head in agreement. 'Me nephew Billy is grave-digger over there; mind you ee'll have some brave old job in all this bleddy rain!'

As if on cue, a squall of rain beat against the windows of the White Horse. The small gathering of old men leaned in towards the comfort of the now crackling fire, away from the coldness of rain and the thought of the graveyard over the river.

Across the Prior's Bridge at nearby St. Thomas churchyard, a grave was being dug by a man dressed in mud, with sacking covering his head and shoulders. As he dug, cursing in the foul weather, the grave started to fill with water.

'Poor bugger,' he muttered viciously to himself. 'Being buried, you could say, for the second time!' He continued digging, his spade squelching in the mire, 'But I'm afeard 'is coffin'll be floating, when 'tis lowered into 'is final resting place.'

Chapter 27.

The time had passed and it was getting near to the festive season. The torrential rain of November had ceased, so the cattle did not look so miserable and sodden in the low-lying pastures which were draining at long last. Eddie Harvey had lain in his watery grave for some weeks now; as the grave-digger at St. Thomas had muttered to himself, he had been buried for the second time.

It had become colder, swirling mists and frosts lying in the valley, making work for the navvies an even harder task, with chapped hands and cracked lips. It was back-breaking hard graft.

However up in the town, the market was in full swing for it would be Christmas soon. Geese which had been fattened up, cackled in their wooden pens, and the butter market was doing good trade. Cattle for sale stood hock-deep in straw, one bullock bellowing loudly, its breath clear to see in the cold morning air. The inns and public houses were busy too, log fires blazing cheerfully to welcome people in from the cold air.

The shops were making the most of the pre-Christmas rush, and the milliner's shop in the square was full of the more prosperous ladies of the town looking for winter bonnets or pretty lace caps, or gloves of kid and silk. In the midst, perched straight-backed on the only elegant chair, was Elizabeth King. Behind her stood her maid, nervously holding various packets and parcels, petrified she might drop some of them.

Elizabeth had not visited the town of Launceston so often since the awful scene with 'that fat common woman' in the square tussling over hat-trimmings some months ago. She was still smarting under all her finery, that she, Miss Elizabeth King of Tregeare, should have been made such an object of ridicule by the local peasants, as she called them. But now in the run-up to Christmas which was a busy period of parties and church services, she needed to replenish her winter bonnets and accessories to show off her exquisite taste and make the most of her family's money. She had already ordered expensive gowns of velvet and taffeta some weeks beforehand, so that she felt sure she would look quite magnificent over the festive season.

Outside the milliner's shop stood Jasper King. He was on strict instructions from his father to stay within calling distance of his sister and he knew this time he must keep a close eye on her, however annoying it was to hang about outside ladies' shops in the cold. His relationship with Elizabeth had not really improved since the summer, but he grudgingly accompanied her on any visits when his father laid down the law. He still thought of her as spoilt and simpering, but that was mostly the fault of his own parents who just could not refuse their eldest daughter anything in the material sense, or it seemed to him.

Jasper stood blowing on his hands, for he had rather stupidly left his leather gloves in the carriage with Ned. People pushed past on the pavements, jostling each other in a happy, cheery manner. Country voices were raised in friendly greeting wishing each other the compliments of the season, for they knew that Christmas was just round the corner. Giggling girls passed by, looking coyly at the rather handsome young man in fine clothes standing outside Miss Fanny's, the milliners. Wagons trundled slowly past, to their allotted places near the church of St. Mary's. Then the town's brass band started up on the corner of the market-place, playing a carol, so that the atmosphere seemed even more festive and a few flakes of sleet or snow even drifted across the square. But where, Jasper mused, in all this winter scene of celebration was the lovely Kate Polglaze? Surely she was not closeted away with her ailing aunt at Werrington, like some kind of nun? Or was she even now in the Infirmary, at the bedside of some young navvy holding his one good hand?

A sudden blast of cold wind made Jasper shiver. Or was it the mere thought of Kate holding someone's hand, when all he really wanted was for her to be touching him instead? Jasper swore under his breath and received a glare from two elderly ladies with purple noses to match their purple bonnets, who were just opening the door and about to enter the inviting warmth of the milliner's.

'Dear Lord they're ugly,' he thought, then felt guilty for his uncharitable thoughts.

The bell tinkled once again and Elizabeth's maid came out nervously, with a message. His sister would be at least an hour, probably more. Jasper could leave his position as a door post outside the shop to fill his time to his own advantage. The maid, who blushed to meet Jasper's dark eyes, bobbed a quick curtsey and darted back inside.

'Excellent!' Jasper needed no more telling, plunging into the crowded market in search of companionship and perhaps a drink or two to celebrate the imminent season of Christmas.

Across the square Kate Polglaze was helping her frail-looking aunt into the trap with their parcels, to return to Werrington. Aunt Nell was exhausted after doing some essential shopping in the busy town, for these days she rarely left the comfort of her home at the farm. Kate tucked a warm rug around her aunt and the trap started off homewards with a jolt, down towards the castle wall. Kate watched it go with some concern, for she was staying on for some further Christmas shopping.

'Ah Miss Polglaze… Kate!' She recognised the voice immediately and swivelled to face its owner.

'Mr. King,' she smiled at him, quite boldly.

'Jasper, please,' he murmured. 'It is some time since we last met.'

'Yes in the Infirmary.' She smiled again, a sudden brilliant smile, at the picture in her mind of his obvious discomfiture at seeing her at the bedside of the injured navvy.

'I hope the young man is now much improved.' God, why was he trembling suddenly, lacking his usual confidence when talking to a woman! That was all she was, a young woman. But as he looked at her with her eyes sparkling in the festive lights dotted around the square, he knew that there was something special beginning between the two of them. Their eyes said it all.

Kate began to tell him about poor Thomas Martock's slow, gradual improvement, but it was obvious to her that Jasper's mind was not really on the same subject. He just could not take his eyes off her, taking in her natural beauty, watching her lips moving as she replied mechanically in medical terms. He was groaning silently inside, as he simply wanted to sweep her dramatically into his arms just like the hero in some of the highly-coloured romantic novels his mother secretly read.

He knew he could be as proud and arrogant as his father when he wanted to be, but in front of this lovely young woman he felt very different.

They were being jostled by the crowds, but neither seemed to notice. Jasper tried to pull himself together and suggested she could have lunch with him in the warmth of the White Hart, with his sister of course, for it would not be acceptable for them to be alone together. Kate's startled expression reflected her concern at this, but Jasper hurriedly poured oil on troubled waters by saying that Elizabeth had not really made a good start to any possible friendship (if it could ever be called that) with Kate on the last occasion. But it was nearly Christmas after all was said and done. It was a time to make merry, and be at peace with all men, or women, perhaps? It would make him so very happy to have her company.

An hour or so later Jasper congratulated himself that he was sitting at a table in the busy White Hart, with his beautifully-dressed sister Elizabeth, who looked as if she had just sucked a lemon, and Kate Polglaze, her eyes still sparkling from the cold air outside.

Now, all that he had to do was to encourage these two very different young women to get on with each other. It would not be an easy task.

Chapter 28.

The conversation at their table was certainly strained at first. Elizabeth could not forget that this same young woman, Kate Polglaze, had shouted an obscenity about cows' muck back at her after their first meeting, as she had climbed into the waiting trap from Werrington Park. It was another poisonous arrow aimed towards her, not easily forgotten, along with the physical attack by the fat common woman in the town square. But Jasper had warned her earlier to be nice, to be friendly towards this Kate person, with her rather unfashionable clothes and her abundant, wild black hair. It was important to him, he'd said sternly, as he'd steered her by the arm from the milliner's. He sounded more like her father in a bad mood with the servants, than her own brother. So, she would tolerate this Kate person at lunch to please him. After all Elizabeth knew this was an opportunity to be admired in one of her many new winter outfits, and she still needed Jasper to be her chaperone on occasions.

Kate meanwhile was enjoying the cheerful fire and the buzz of many voices, laughing and shouting their compliments of the season across the room. It was a happy, relaxed scene and she was determined to make the most of it! There wasn't much laughter or celebrating at Werrington these days; her cousin Jack was forever working or monosyllabic at meal-times, while her aunt was like a timid little mouse quietly scuttling round the place. It would be a strange Christmas this year.

Glasses of mulled wine arrived, to warm them, the sweet scent of cinnamon wafted over the table. Holly and ivy decorated the granite lintel over the fireplace, the red berries glistening in the light from the flickering flames. Jasper began to unwind, the wine warming him. He simply could not believe his luck sitting across the table from Kate, being able to watch her, to talk to her, after so many months.

Elizabeth sipped her mulled wine in lady-like fashion, observing Jasper over the rim of the wine-glass and his obvious fascination for this unusual young woman. She had seen her brother so many times being pursued at parties by women, some of them very rich and some much older and experienced, and noted Jasper's high-handed attitude towards them. But this was different. She narrowed her eyes like a cat as she watched the pair, their eyes shining brightly as they both laughed at some little thing or other.

Golden-skinned roast capon was served, accompanied by a decanter of fine white wine which Jasper had chosen carefully. Kate enjoyed being presented with delicious food, rather than having to resurrect something her aunt had burnt or vegetables which had been left to boil dry. The conversation was rather stilted with Elizabeth, but if she was aloof then at least she was not impolite. They did not touch on the building of the railway line this time, and Elizabeth's great aversion to navvies. Jasper remembered the animosity last time on the subject between her and Kate, and to be honest he was sick to death of hearing people argue about the advantages and disadvantages of the new line out towards Egloskerry and on to the North coast. This was often followed by the usual sniping about the unruly behaviour of the navvies and how some of them had been accused of poaching and other such criminal actions.

Elizabeth regaled them with tales of the latest fashions in London, and Kate tried to look interested in talk of ball-gowns and brocade, velvet drapery and silk shawls, for when would she require such things? She imagined herself feeding Aunt Nell's poultry in such glorious clothes and could not help herself smiling at the picture!

Jasper gave Kate an encouraging look, as if he sensed her thoughts. He launched into an anecdote about a recent foxhunt held on the Tregeare Estate, and his great love of horses shone through as he talked of an accident when someone's hunter had jumped awkwardly and had to be shot. His dark brown eyes were misty as he related the tale, and Elizabeth's unfeeling comment that horses were easily replaced made him look at her with something like hatred in those same eyes.

'And what about you, Miss Polglaze? Do you ride?' Elizabeth arranged her cutlery neatly on the plate as she spoke.

'Kate.' She took a deep breath, 'Yes I love to ride, but it's hard at the moment to fit it in, what with my aunt being unwell... and with my work at the Infirmary.'

'Work?' Elizabeth's blue eyes widened, incredulous.

'Yes, I am a volunteer nurse at the Infirmary.' Kate picked up her wine-glass, sipped a tiny mouthful, and smiled across the table.

'You actually work? For money?' Elizabeth's icy voice showed clearly her total disapproval.

'It is very rewarding, helping those who are sick and in pain... and no, I don't receive any payment, Elizabeth. I am a volunteer.'

Jasper cleared his throat in the following silence. 'Well I think it's wonderful Miss Polglaze. Kate.' His voice softened. 'To do something so sacrificial for the poor people of Launceston. It cannot be an easy task at times.'

There was still an uneasy atmosphere and as they had finished eating, Jasper beckoned the serving-girl over. Elizabeth had barely touched her food, but Kate's plate was almost empty. She had eaten with relish, no silly picking at this and that like a spoilt child.

The plates were taken away and Jasper poured more wine and took a huge mouthful. Kate could see that he was suffering on account of his sister. Elizabeth had become silent, her mouth like a painted doll's, shut up tightly. Her mind was ticking over. She could not wait to tell her father that Jasper appeared to be falling in love with a girl from a farm, who actually worked in the Infirmary!

A joyous shout from across the room, which had suddenly become unbearably hot, roused the three of them from their private thoughts. Jasper's friend from school-days, Isaac Penhale, pushed his way through the people towards them.

Smiling as always, in what looked like a new coat and cravat, Isaac slapped Jasper on his back, before turning his attention to the ladies. 'Miss King! How splendidly fashionable you look!' She simpered at the compliment.

Finally he turned to Kate. 'And who might this lovely lady be Jasper?'

This was obviously the young woman living at Werrington, who Jasper was infatuated with. And no wonder! She was really quite exotic-looking, with wild black curls tumbling down onto a rather plain gown. This then was the girl with no fortune.

'Draw up a chair Isaac, let me get another decanter of wine!' Jasper greeted him warmly. 'How is life out at Basil Manor? Your mother is well I hope. And Sir Isaac, your father?'

Elizabeth's pale cheeks flushed at the mention of the title of rank.

'My father is sadly most unwell Jasper.' Isaac's face became gloomy. 'He spends most of his days in bed these days, too weak to get on his horse to attend to our estate. Mother is resigned to having a sick husband it seems, and she waits on him from dawn till dusk.'

Kate murmured her sadness to hear such news, for she had immediately found Isaac Penhale to be a friendly, likeable young man. Elizabeth's blue eyes did not betray her own train of thought, which was occupied with the idea of her brother's friend becoming a baronet, Sir Isaac Penhale of Basil Manor, before very much longer.

The time passed quite pleasantly and even Elizabeth thawed and joined in the conversation, without alluding to her expensive new muff of mink, which would have been a sure conversation-killer.

When the lad from Werrington came to announce the trap was waiting outside the White Hart, Kate's departure was quite civilised compared with the previous occasion. There was no mention of cows at all, or their inevitable cow pats, and even Elizabeth seemed quite gracious in her farewell. After all, one has to be gracious if one is suddenly dreaming, or scheming, of becoming the next Lady of the Manor! Isaac said a friendly goodbye, smiling broadly, and wished Kate the compliments of the season.

But Jasper could not bear for Kate to leave. All he really wanted at that moment was to hold her close to him in an embrace. It would most likely be after the Christmas period before they would meet again.

He helped her up into the trap, the air cold and frosty now after the warmth of the White Hart. The market was packing up and the townsfolk were hurrying home in the growing darkness.

'Merry Christmas Kate,' his voice was husky with emotion. He watched as the Werrington trap made its way down towards the castle walls and beyond.

Chapter 29

It was Christmas Eve and darkness had fallen. Grey-faced navvies trooped along the Kensey valley homeward-bound. Not that these men had real homes, most had been used to living in shanty settlements all over the country, so for some their current lodgings with Cornish families were comfortable, if a little cramped! The younger men were loud, excitable, looking forward to an evening celebrating in the local hostelries with their Christmas pay-packets. The older married men among them just wanted a break from the sheer hell of the hard work, to spend some time with their families and to eke out their money enough to enjoy the festive season.

In the higher pastures above the old Deer Park, sheep could be heard bleating in the darkness, a reminder of the shepherds in the Holy Land tending their flocks all those hundreds of years ago. The light of a silvery moon appeared, bathing all in the valley below in moon-blanched tones.

In shacks and cottages near the Tannery down at Riverside, the navvies washed the dust and dirt away as best they could, their scrawny children huddling by firesides. There the sticks and wood which they had picked up out Underlane in the fields earlier that day, spat and crackled. As they looked into the dancing flames, they whispered excitedly of Christmas Day, and the presents they hoped to receive from old Father Christmas himself if they were lucky. Maybe something exotic like an orange each, or a small bag of nuts to share. In damp sculleries worn-looking women took a secretive drop o' gin with hot water, more often than not in chipped cups, toasting the fact that they, and their families, had survived another hard year, their husbands working their guts out to build the new stretch of railway line. A few of the navvies spared a thought for their work-mate Eddie, now lying cold and dead in the churchyard near the river. They remembered his laughing face, his small acts of kindness and his love of life. There would be little cause for celebration for his widow and children this Christmas-tide.

The Vicar of St. Thomas dunked his biscuit in his tea, sitting alone in his echoing vicarage like a vault, and thought of how he could inspire the people with his words at the coming Midnight Mass. The faithful would be there in crowds, the candles flickering in the gloom on the altar and on window-ledges. The bell would toll in the darkness and the carved granite faces on the Norman font would be illuminated by the candle-light and stare blankly out, as they had done since the days of the peaceful monks and the Priory. He mused on the passage of time and how the world was changing, with the building of the new railway line from Launceston and the drinking and fighting of its workers. No doubt the inns and public houses up in the town would be over-flowing with navvies and hard-drinking men, spending their money on the demon drink instead of feeding their families. He sighed and finished the dregs of his cooling tea with its remnants of soggy biscuit at the bottom of his cup.

At Werrington a few miles away, Kate was sitting by the fire in its huge granite fireplace, dreaming as she stared at the flames and the glowing red caves among the burning logs. Her aunt was sitting quietly at the table reading the Family Bible by lamp-light before taking herself off to bed. Kate's cousin Jack was snoring his head off like a raging bull, by the blazing fire, in what had once been his father's old armchair. This was a different Christmas here too. Last year Kate had been at home, down Cornwall, with her busy, chaotic family. Then she had come to stay with her Aunt Nell on the farm for a while but when her Uncle Tom had been taken ill and died so suddenly, leaving seemed out of the question. Her aunt had come to depend on her over the months, and her monosyllabic cousin seemed to accept that Kate would stay on to help his mother, who was as timid as a mouse, and obviously not coping well with her bereavement. But in that time Kate's life had changed in other ways. She had struck out for some sort of independence in her voluntary work at the Infirmary, seeing things she had not imagined in her limited experience. She had watched old men die, and she had seen vibrant young men, like the injured navvy Thomas Martock, seriously injured and facing a very bleak, different future. If she had but known it, in twenty years' time those same hospital beds would be full of dying and injured young men sent home from the battlefields of the Great War. Also in her time living at Werrington, Kate had met Jasper King of Tregeare House. And, despite her better judgement, she was drawn to him more and more.

If Kate Polglaze was sparing a thought of Jasper King that Christmas Eve, then Mary-Jane Jenkin at Badharlick was thinking of her William, as she had come to call him in her mind. William Treglown was never very far from her thoughts, as she milked the cows or scoured out the milk pans in the dairy, or even when she was turning the handle of the butter churn.

This Christmas would be different she knew, as her own family at Killicoff had given lodgings to what seemed at times like hordes of navvies. Most of them were working near the ill-fated Red Down or Riddon cutting where the land-slip had occurred, but some of the other men in the village were sawyers providing cut timber for the bridge being constructed near New Mills. Whatever they were, Mary Jane resented these strange men living so closely with her family.

She hated their loud voices with different dialects. But most of all she hated their confidence, probably due to their being used to living in many different parts of the country. Anyway she must not dwell on it, for it was Christmas Eve, and soon she would be walking in from the farm at Badharlick with the other workers to partake in the Christmas Midnight Mass at St. Keri's church.

It was a cold, clear evening and their breath smoked on the air as they walked the couple of miles to the church, laughing and talking animatedly. To their right, the dark outline of Riddon loomed threateningly in the distance, but the lane ahead was like a silver ribbon twisting and turning towards the village of Egloskerry. Stars shone in the velvety dark sky ahead of them and one seemed to shine out more brightly than any other.

'See that star up there?' Old Sarah stopped in her tracks and puffed heavily as she spoke. 'Tes like the star shining over the stable at Bethlehem.'

A murmur of voices assented.

'Well I d'reckon tis hanging o'er Farmer Paul's piggeries!' The creaky voice and comment of Jan Higgins, one of the Badharlick farm labourers, made them all collapse in infectious laughter for one or two had already supped some cider secretly in the barn before their outing. Only old Sarah was grim-faced.

'Tis bad of 'ee to laugh at such, on this holiest night of all nights!' She stumped on ahead of them, puffing and wheezing, clearly offended by their mockery.

'Don't 'ee take on so Sarah,' Jan called after her. 'They shepherds watching their flocks by night in the Good Book were only 'oomans, like what we be.'

The laughter subsided and the group walked on up the lane towards the village of Egloskerry. As they approached the church by the main gate, they could see its windows lit by flickering candles.

'Tis some picturesque!' Mary Jane's admiring voice could be heard as they made their way towards the porch.

'And where did 'ee get a big word like that then Mary Jane?' Old Sarah whispered in her ear. 'From your sweetheart William Treglown, I'll be bound.'

There was no time to reply, for the men were taking off their hats and they were being ushered into the pews. The little church of St. Keri was soon packed with local people searching for spiritual inspiration for it was Christmas night, and the service of Holy Communion began.

Mary Jane thought of all the men and women who had prayed here over the hundreds of years. As always her eyes were drawn to a helmet with a visor and gauntlets which always fascinated, and yet frightened her. She had once been told that the armour had come from the armoury at Penheale Manor and was worn in the English Civil War by Sir John Somebody or other. She wished, not for the first time, that she was more learned.

She noticed her family squeezed in at the back of the church in the shadows, her poor mother looking so tired and worn that Mary Jane wanted to push her way through the people to simply put her arms around her, to comfort her.

After the service was over the congregation started to make their way out into the cold, star-studded night. Mary Jane spent a few precious moments talking to her mother and her excited brothers and sisters, and then she realised she had been left behind. The Badharlick folk had already disappeared into the dark lanes without her.

Clutching her thick woollen shawl tightly around her, she began to run down the lane towards Badharlick Bridge to catch up with her friends, her breath puffing out in white wispy clouds around her.

Mary Jane did not see the man following her, slinking along in the shadows of the hedgerows. The first thing she knew of him, was when he caught her from behind and with his hand clamped tightly over her mouth dragged her into the deeper darkness of the overhanging trees.

She struggled vainly, but he was simply too strong for her. When she twisted and turned, scratching at his face, clawing at his eyes with her fingernails, he smashed his clenched fist into her face to shut her up. Breathing heavily now, his stale breath smelt of cider and ale. Then he threw her to the ground which felt cold and hard beneath her. He tore at her layers of skirts and petticoats, laughing at her feeble attempts to defend herself from his attack.

'I've wanted to do this for some time,' he whispered triumphantly into her ear, his voice was muffled and yet it seemed vaguely familiar.

She looked up as he put all his weight on her, pinning her down under him so easily.

High above in the heavens she could see the stars silently shining, for this was Christmas Eve, a holy night.

The hot tears welled over her bruised and bloodied face. Mary Jane's strength had gone, any struggle was futile. Her body simply gave up the fight and it was not hers any more...

Chapter 30.

Tregeare House was waking up to Christmas Day, its chimneys smoking in the cold light of day. A frost lay across the broad sweeping lawns and the water in the granite horse-troughs had frozen solid. Above the distant trees a faint rose-pink colour washed the sky creating a scene of breath-taking beauty.

The house-maids had risen early to light the fires in the Library and the dining room downstairs and now they tiptoed up to the galleried landing with its fluted ionic columns to the numerous bedrooms and dressing rooms. They struggled up the impressive staircase as quietly as possible with pails of kindling and brushes to sweep the hearths, so the King family would not have to wash and dress in the bitter cold.

Jasper had also woken early. He had lain in his bed luxuriating in the warmth and comfort, thinking of the past months and how his mind had changed on a lot of things since meeting Kate Polglaze. He admired her strength of character, as well as her untamed beauty. She did not need the fripperies of other women, in fact seeing her in a plain dress seemed to show off her natural beauty even more! He smiled to think of his own shock when he had first seen her in her white voluntary nurse's outfit in the Infirmary, her wild black hair hidden by a simple white headscarf. But his smile faded when he thought of her sitting at the bedside of that navvy Martock, even holding his one good hand. A stab of jealousy went through him suddenly, though he knew it was absolutely bloody ridiculous! How could he be jealous of a navvy, and an injured one at that, who would probably never see clearly again and who was waking up this Christmas morning with only one good arm? Kate had certainly woken Jasper from his drowsy state of disinterest in women. Well that was not entirely true, he had always liked women but it was more a case of seeing how quickly he could get to seduce them, or even in the case of one or two pretty serving girls enjoy a tumble in the hay with them! But that had all changed. He had realised, in this gradual awakening, that the beautiful Kate Polglaze was the only woman he'd ever really wanted. She was an extraordinary woman, and she deserved to be treated with respect.

A beam of pinkish-golden light gleamed through the tiny gap between the expensive brocade curtains which adorned the tall twelve-pane sash window of his bedroom. Jasper pushed the heavy covers back and climbed out of the huge bed with its feather mattress. His head was thumping now he was upright and his mouth was dry, both probably the result of too much wine on Christmas Eve! What he needed was to clear the cobwebs away before the rest of the family had roused, for all seemed still quiet and calm in the elegant old house.

Half an hour later, Jasper was trotting down the drive on his chestnut gelding, leaving a dazed-looking stable boy scratching his head as he'd been dragged out of his bed above the stables most unexpectedly to saddle up the horse. But Jasper was intent on getting away from the imminent scenes of excitement and chaos when his younger brothers and sisters awoke to Christmas morning. The cold, crisp air was stimulating him as he moved in time with the rhythmic motion of the animal beneath him, squeezing with his knees urging the horse on across the parkland.

By the time that Jasper returned from his bracing ride, the hang-over from the night before had vanished and he felt uplifted. The mere sight of the Palladian architecture of their beautiful house stirred his emotions as he approached on horseback, thinking once again how lucky he and his family were to live in such a wonderful place.

The family were by now up and about having breakfasted, and they would soon be preparing to go to Laneast church that morning for their Christmas communion. Jasper kissed his mother fondly on her head, as she sat contentedly by the fire in the Library, drinking tea, and watching her younger children playing with some of their expensive-looking Christmas gifts. He could imagine how lovely she must have looked when she was a younger woman, but now after giving birth to so many children she was putting on weight.

There was, of course no sign yet of his sister Elizabeth, who was probably still sifting through her expensive winter wardrobe of newly-made velvet gowns, piles of petticoats and basque jackets to find something stunning to wear to church. She loved that moment of drama when heads turned as she walked down the aisle behind her parents. She could hear the loud whispers coming from the wives and daughters in their sensible, church-going outfits, as she wafted past with her head held high in the air looking simply glorious.

Well, Jasper thought, Elizabeth had better come up with something warm to wear, as the damp old church was usually freezing cold. It was best to dress for comfort. But he knew that Elizabeth only wanted to dazzle! As if on cue, the double doors to the Library opened and there was his sister, dressed stylishly and with a tiny, wispy winter bonnet. In her gloved hands she clutched her prayer book. The whole effect was very pretty he had to admit, and for one fleeting moment he wondered what his dear friend Isaac Penhale would think... for his sister had flirted with him outrageously at their lunch in the White Hart! Yet Jasper had the distinct feeling it was more to do with his ailing father's title, rather than anything else.

Philip King was the last to enter the Library that Christmas morning, and like his daughter he was immaculately dressed. A diamond pin glinted on his snowy cravat. He was smiling at the scene which confronted him, congratulating himself on his fine-looking family and his elegant home. He made a mental note that in the New Year he must obtain the services of an artist to create a painting of just such a scene, to hang in the hall below the impressive staircase.

Jasper had been right about St. Sidwell's church. It was bitterly cold, perishing even, inside the ancient building. But it was packed full of farmers and families, their children far too cold to wriggle about in their pews. The Kings had made their usual grand entrance, escorted to their pew at the front by an ancient, tottering church warden. Elizabeth revelled in the moment, dreaming, as the eyes of the seated congregation swivelled towards her. How she would love it when she became the next Lady Penhale, nodding graciously at the peasants from her husband's manorial estate as she swept past them in all her glory!

After the service the King family did not waste much time getting into the two waiting carriages, as the cold had penetrated their very bones whilst in the church, or so it seemed to them.

'Thank the Lord that Great-uncle did not ramble on too long in the pulpit about the Virgin Birth today,' Jasper muttered under his breath to no-one in particular as he climbed into one of the carriages.

Elizabeth was already seated inside, arranging her plum-coloured velvet skirts artistically.

'What exactly is a Virgin Birth?' piped up their ten-year-old brother John innocently, who was squeezing into their carriage for the journey home and trying to avoid sitting on his sister Elizabeth's skirts.

'Not today old chap. No difficult questions today,' Jasper smirked as he turned his head away to look out of the carriage window. Elizabeth took a sudden intake of breath, sniffed loudly in a most un-ladylike fashion and bent her head to search in her tiny bag for a lace handkerchief, so John had to be content. The two younger children were soon chattering away about Christmas presents, blissfully unaware of such unanswerable questions.

The dining-room at Tregeare House had never looked so welcoming. Enormous log fires were blazing away at each end of the room and the long dining table looked absolutely beautiful with its pristine tablecloth and napkins, gleaming silver cutlery and crystal wine glasses. In the centre of the table, arrangements of holly and Christmas roses had been placed artistically amidst the flickering candles. Jasper's mother smiled with satisfaction. Luncheon was served and it was delicious, even her husband Philip King seemed to have no reason to complain or be bad tempered on such a day.

Later they retired to the Library with its shining mirrors and polished bookcases. Philip looked around him. He was enjoying Christmas Day surrounded by his family and he was doing well in the world. Yes there were worries about business or the estate at times, but today was not the day to dwell on them. He poured another glass of red wine and held it up, so it was glowing in the firelight. In the New Year he would have a heart-to-heart with his son, Jasper, and make it plain that he must start looking for a suitable wife. She would be a young woman from an excellent family, with style and sophistication. She would be someone who would be an asset to the Tregeare Estate, bringing in an ample dowry. Money would be the key.

Philip King had been brought up in a moderately wealthy family with a background in the cloth trade, a business in tailoring and stay-making. The family had owned property too, cottages and houses at Newport, a farm at South Petherwin, as well as a fine house in Southgate Street where Philip Gidley King himself had been born. But now Philip King wanted, (nay demanded even), a lot more for his own offspring. Tregeare House had already cost him a small fortune!

He looked across at his handsome son, who was talking animatedly to his mother while they played cards. Anne doted on him, Philip knew to his cost. But then he caught sight of Elizabeth, draped prettily by the Library fire, his favourite daughter in her beautiful clothes. It would not be too long before a marriage would be arranged for her too. But it would have to be someone really special to be good enough for his Elizabeth; he swallowed a mouthful of his wine and his eyes narrowed, he could hardly bear to think of daily life at Tregeare without her.

Elizabeth looked up suddenly, feeling her father's eyes on her. She smiled at him, and giggled. In a silly little girl's voice, which suggested she had drunk perhaps too much wine as was good for a young lady, 'Did you know Father dear, that my brother Jasper has fallen in love?' She paused. 'The lady in question's quite beautiful in a wild sort of way... but she's said to be penniless.'

Philip's face drained of all colour but Elizabeth continued relentlessly, warming to her theme, 'And I do believe she works in the Infirmary in Launceston!'

The laughter and chatter in the room seemed to slow and stop suddenly, even the younger children playing with their toys went quiet as if they knew any noise might mean trouble from their father.

Philip King had become grey and bleak-looking, like a statue carved out of the local moorland granite. He stood amidst the wreckage of all his plans and dreams of securing an heiress for his eldest son, Jasper.

Outside the tall windows, flakes of snow started to drift down very softly in the darkness.

Chapter 31.

After her assailant had vanished into the black velvety night on Christmas Eve, Mary Jane had lain still on the hard earth. Her eyes opened and above her she could see the cold, distant stars still shining down as before. In the near distance, Riddon would be a black outline looming against the starry night. Nothing had changed. Yet everything had changed in her world.

She touched her face tentatively with her finger-tips. It was swollen and bleeding where he had punched her. Her whole body was wracked with pain and shaking in the cold; she knew that she must either get up, or simply close her eyes and die there, frozen under the trees.

Was this how William had felt after the brutal attack on him, when he was left for dead in a deep ditch at Little Athill?

At the thought of William, tears of self-pity welled up again in Mary Jane's eyes. She must not think of him. She must never think of him again. No more would she share secret stolen kisses with him at Badharlick Bridge, for she was ruined. Damaged goods, was the way some of the gossipy village women described it. She had overheard them in the Post Office, when a girl from Egloskerry had got herself in the family way. It was her own fault, they'd said cruelly. She'd asked for it. Mary Jane groaned as she tried to move slightly. Is that how they would talk of her one day? Was the man never to blame?

Gradually she managed to push herself up into a sitting position. She waited, breathless, then she dragged herself up even more, with the help of an overhanging branch. Her clothes were dishevelled and torn and in the moonlight she could see a trickle of what must be blood, black and sticky like treacle, on her white skin.

It took her a long time to stagger up the lane to the farm at Badharlick. She felt her physical strength had all gone and that she was bent over like an old woman, struggling to make her limbs work after the violence wrought upon her. Yet all around the scene was one of peace in nature. Pure light was pouring from the moon. Hundreds, no thousands, of stars were shining beautifully in the heavens above. Sheep were lying out in the fields clustering against the tall hedges; she could smell the flock, and she could hear a couple of ewes bleating soft and low and in the night. Soon there would be new lambs born into the world...

'Lamb of God,' she whispered some words of the service of Holy Communion to herself, as she struggled along in her pain. 'That takest away the sins of the world... have mercy upon us.'

She thought once again, of the pretty milkmaid Charlotte Dymond, who had been attacked out on the lonely moorland at Roughtor some forty or fifty years before. Had she fought with her assailant, like Mary Jane? Or had she known him? The man, who went on to slit her throat. He had left her poor body in her best Sunday clothes, by the stream, while curlews cried mournfully and buzzards hung high overhead. Nature had not come to her help.

She clung to the granite gate-post of the farm when she eventually reached Badharlick, as if it was an old friend. A lamp still flickered in the kitchen window, its yellow light cast out onto the frozen muck of the farmyard making it look like a sugary bread pudding. The horse trough was frozen solid. Yet in the east there was a faint glimmer of light, for the birth of Christmas Day. She lifted the heavy latch to the door and staggered inside the old farmhouse. Thank God no-one had pushed the heavy metal bolts across, for denied access would surely have killed her. As she pulled open the kitchen door, she felt the warmth still emanating from the embers in the huge fireplace and she moved thankfully towards it, seeking comfort. She knelt down gingerly on the hearth, her white, frozen hands held out towards the last vestiges of warmth.

The voice made her start. Old and croaky, as if the owner had not spoken for some time. It came from one of the high-backed settles.

'And where do y' think you've been, out till this late hour Mary Jane Jenkin?' Sarah's tired, wrinkled face could just be seen, peering out of the shadows, yawning.

She could see the girl turn, startled. In the lamp-light, could see her swollen and bruised face.

'My dear Lord!' Old Sarah left her place under a blanket on the settle. 'What on earth has happened to 'ee, chiel?' The horror could be heard in her voice.

'Help me, Sarah,' the girl's voice breaking with emotion, as the tears started to fill her eyes, despite herself.

The old woman helped her up from her knees and looked into the girl's smashed face: her lips swollen, one eye blackened, dried blood on her cheek and mouth. Then her gaze travelled down over Mary Jane's clothes, took in the torn bodice and skirt, the filthy petticoats. For once in her long life, Sarah was speechless.

She took the girl into her arms then and rocked her, like one would a child. She was stroking her hair, rocking her gently, shushing her tears away. When Mary Jane eventually pulled away, Sarah helped her to the settle and tucked the blanket round her trembling body. She picked up the poker and stirred some life into the fire, throwing on dry sticks and logs. Gradually flames licked hungrily around them and lit up the cavernous fireplace.

Sarah quietly went about her work, fetching a bowl of water and a soft piece of flannel. She gently washed the girl's face and shaking body, sponging away the dried blood, not speaking, not asking the obvious questions. She carefully and slowly climbed up the creaking stairs, returning with a warm nightgown and shawl. Wrapped in her comforting blanket, Mary Jane was sleeping the sleep of the exhausted. She would leave her for a while... but not for too long, or the household would soon be waking up to celebrate the coming of Christmas.

The old woman sat brooding by the fire, wondering what Devil's work had taken place somewhere between the village and the farmstead at Badharlick. The girl was in a bad way, that was obvious. Not only was her face damaged, it looked as if some man, or men, had ripped her clothes and had their evil way with her! But who would do such a terrible thing hereabouts?

William Treglown's face appeared in her muddled old head, but she would not believe it of him. He was a fine young man, with a caring, gentle nature. William was Mary Jane's sweetheart, surely.

Then, who? Who, in the surrounding Egloskerry area, would attack an innocent young girl in such a violent way?

As the morning light started to filter through the kitchen windows, the germ of an idea dawned in Sarah's mind. Bleddy Navvies! There were hated navvies everywhere these days, in Egloskerry. It must have been one of those demons. A man with no respect for anyone, or anything.

The light became stronger. She must stir her old stumps. She must wake Mary Jane and help her up the stairs and out the way darned quickly. She certainly wasn't in a fit state to encounter the enquiring looks and endless questions of her workmates.

Sarah sighed to herself as she heaved herself to her feet. She was exhausted and shocked by the night's terrible events.

'What a way to greet Christmas Day!'

Chapter 32.

It was early on the day after Christmas Day and up at Tregeare House the gentle fall of snow had melted and simply disappeared. As it was Boxing Day, and the Feast of St. Stephen, the household staff were mulling over the contents of their 'boxes' from their employers, the King family, who were nowhere to be seen at this hour of the day. An uneasy atmosphere lay over the house, with much whispering amongst the housemaids and kitchen maids behind the green baize door and down in the kitchens. They knew that something dramatic had happened the evening before in the Library, for the double doors had swung open suddenly and violently before Philip King, the Master, had emerged with a face like thunder. He had stalked across the echoing hall, decanter of brandy in hand, before shutting himself in his study and nearly taking the door off its hinges in the process!

At the end of what had been a perfect day up till then, the family gathering had gradually dispersed, melting away like the flakes of snow outside. The young children had been hustled away up to bed by the nanny, away from their mother, whose once beautiful face had been showing all the signs of despair and distress. She too had been seen by the spying servants soon afterwards, walking rather wearily up the staircase towards the sanctuary of her bedroom, the rustling skirts of her silken dress trailing behind her. Only Jasper King and his sister Elizabeth had remained in the Library and before long, voices had been raised.

Jasper's deep voice could be heard clearly venting his spleen at his sister, and the listening housemaids had never heard such language coming from the young Master!

'He were in a right old tizz, I'm telling you,' whispered Rosie, after checking to see that none of the family was somewhere listening. 'The names he called Miss Elizabeth… well, I don't suppose they'd even be allowed in the public houses on market day!'

'What like?' Daisy, the scullery girl, moved closer to Rosie, desperate to hear more. 'What sort of names?'

Rosie looked behind her again, before she took an intake of breath and blurted out, 'He called her a venomous slut!'

'Ohhh my dear Lord…' Daisy's wide-open eyes showed her shock and disbelief. 'Rosie… What's venomous mean?'

'It means she's poison,' a man's voice made them jump apart, trembling. He was carrying a wicker basket of logs in from the cold outside.

'But we all d'know that.' He dumped the basket heavily down on the scrubbed floor near the range. 'She's nort but a spoilt brat when it comes down to it.' Then he left the kitchen without more ado.

'Tis a good job they upstairs never heard Tom say that,' said Rosie quietly. 'Or he'd be down the road, looking for another place to work, even if 'tis St. Stephen's Feast and still Christmas.'

'But 'tis true what he said, fer all that!' Daisy tried to smother her girlish laughter in her apron, pulling it up to her face. Then more sorrowfully she murmured, 'The times Miss Elizabeth have been cruel to me… I can't begin to tell'ee. Shouting and screaming at me, saying how ugly and useless I am. How no-one can bear to be in the kitchen with me, so I have to stay out back in the scullery all the time.'

She wiped hot tears away. Rosie gave the scullery maid a sisterly hug, but there were no words to comfort her. All the servants knew how cruel Elizabeth King could be!

'Anyways,' Rosie announced with vigour, 'we must be getting on with our work before the family is up and about. Tis only a few hours from now that the Tregeare Foxhounds will be having their Meet outside the front of the house! 'Twill be like all hell let loose serving them all drinks and the Lord knows what, if I know anything about it.'

Out in the stable block at the rear of the elegant house, it was already frenetic. The stable boys had been up for hours rising in the darkness, feeding and watering the horses by the light of the flickering stable lamps; grooming the hunters until their coats gleamed, cleaning and polishing saddles and bridles which did not really need it, but they knew their work would be closely scrutinised by the Master himself on this day of all days. Everything must look perfect, and woe betide anyone who was not doing his job to the best of his ability on that day.

As the wintry sun was breaking through the low clouds, the first gentlemen on horseback trotted up the driveway. They were met at the doorway by Philip King himself, immaculately turned out for the hunt and all smiles this morning as if the events of the previous evening had not taken place. Servants were carrying trays of clinking glasses containing mulled wine and spirits for the riders, nervously moving between the horses, which were wheeling around, churning up the mud and gravel with their hooves. There was the friendly smell of horse dung and the metallic clinking of bits. Jasper was obviously avoiding his father for he remained skulking in the stables for as long as possible. Suddenly he emerged, mounted on Midnight, his powerful-looking black stallion.

Up above the Meet, watching the lively scene from her bedroom window was the pale face of his sister, Elizabeth. Ghost-like she drew back against the brocade curtains when Jasper looked up. He had felt that someone was watching him from the upstairs windows... His face hardened as he caught a glimpse of her, and he tipped his head back and swallowed his whisky in one mouthful. It warmed him, burning almost as it went down his gullet. He made meanings towards one of the tray-bearing servants and leaned down to take another glass, his stirrup leathers creaking as he did so. He intended to drink as much as he wanted later on his return from the day's hunting, to obliterate any future interference from his overbearing bloody father!

The pack of foxhounds made its noisy appearance from their nearby kennels, led by the Master of Foxhounds and his helper, the Whipper-in. The busy scene became a swirling mass of excitable, baying hounds, wheeling horses and splashes of scarlet colour. Sitting aloft on his nervously prancing stallion, Jasper surveyed the familiar gathering. Normally he would feel excited at the thought of the day's hunting, but this morning he simply felt angry. Angry at Elizabeth, his thoughtless sister and the way she had maliciously caused the stir which had, in effect, ruined the end of a perfect family Christmas Day. He reached down again to take yet another glass of spirits from a passing servant with a chinking tray. He knew it was sheer madness for he'd had no breakfast, but the whisky made him feel alive, adding fuel to his own fire deep within.

The image of Kate, beautiful Kate Polglaze swam before his eyes. It made him smile ironically, as he briefly met the stony look from his father on his huge bay. As far as Jasper was concerned, the hunt was well and truly on and Kate was his quarry. His bloody father could go hang as far as he was concerned. It would take more than a Whipper-in to keep Jasper King under control and stop him from rebelling.

The Master blew on his hunting horn and the excited hounds began their almost eerie howling. Soon their music would be heard for miles as they chased across the open countryside.

Several hours later, a black stallion cantered wildly back up the drive of Tregeare House, plastered in mud and with its reins flying free. The stable boys caught the dangling reins and attempted to calm the lathered horse. Now there would be trouble at Tregeare, for the stallion's rider had been Jasper King the young Master.

But Jasper was, quite simply, nowhere to be seen.

Chapter 33.

The Iron Horse clanked heavily and hissed out steam as it thundered into the station at Launceston, accompanying the sound of warning bells. Soon it would be well-watered and cared for.

There was bustle as passengers alighted from its carriages, ladies in warm coats and winter hats, one or two gentlemen in top hats from the Railway Company, watched by a smattering of grubby children standing on the iron and wooden bridge. The station was busy and noisy, whistles blowing, porters trundling luggage along the platform, all watched by the station cat sitting in a sunny patch of winter sunshine.

Outside the platform next to the smartly-painted railings were the horse-drawn buses belonging to the hotels, the White Hart and the Castle Temperance awaiting any guests. Others would have to walk up the long hill, or climb Zig-Zag up to Horse Lane.

A rather worn-looking woman in a shabby navy coat was among the passengers who alighted from the train that day. She was the mother of Thomas Martock the injured navy, who was still a patient in the Infirmary up in the town. She had a frightened, rabbity look about her, as she clutched her bag and started the long haul up the winding hill.

Inside the Infirmary, Kate Polglaze was at work, her remarkable black hair hidden by her white headscarf. She was glad to be busy, back at her duties, after the few days spent back on the farm at Werrington. It had been a very quiet Christmas, her aunt's first as a widow. Her cousin

Jack had eaten his fill over the so-called 'festive' period, but he was no company, his monosyllabic replies had all but driven Kate mad, and her Aunt Nell was not much better. She had wept quietly for her dead husband, eating only tiny amounts of food which were not enough to keep a wren alive. Yes, Kate thought, she was glad to be back at work, as she rolled bandages and emptied stinking bedpans into the sluice.

She had thought of Jasper King a lot over the past few days, his handsome face was never very far from her mind. But, she reflected, despite their growing attraction to each other, she must face it. Jasper could not be for her. He was from a different background, expected to make an excellent marriage to someone with pots of money or acres of land, no doubt, to please the rather aloof, grim-faced father she had seen him with on one occasion at the market in the autumn.

She was pleased that the navvy, Thomas Martock, seemed to be making a fairly good recovery all things considered. Of course the loss of an arm was a terrible thing, but there was a whisper going around that he would receive some sort of compensation from the railway company. As for his sight, when the swathes of bandages were removed there had been gradual signs of light and faint outlines of shapes, so that he was no longer in total darkness and despair.

The visit from his mother by train from afar, was also an improvement on her very first sight of her injured son. She had steeled herself to be more positive, to try to uplift her boy so that he knew he had some sort of life to come home to. How she would actually cope on his eventual return, this worn-looking woman, she did not know. But she knew that her continuous weeping at his bedside on her first visit had not done him any favours. That kind nurse with the lovely face had held her hand

and told her to try and be brave, for Thomas's sake. Mrs. Martock had admonished herself for her own behaviour on the long return journey from Launceston, as the steam train had puffed its way through the seemingly endless countryside, smoke and smuts occasionally flying through the partly open window. Kate was pleased to see mother and son talking to each other more calmly this time, and she smiled encouragingly towards them as she passed to and fro, busy with her tasks.

Two elderly male patients were leaning towards each other, talking in hushed tones from their hospital beds as Kate passed by, catching only snippets of their conversation.

'Ess that's what 'ee said,' one whiskered man croaked. 'Twas that there Jasper King, from out Tregeare estate.'

A jolt ran through her. She paused by the next empty bed, pretending to read a medical paper in her hand, yet listening intently.

'What, your grandson works out Tregeare? Niver know'd that afore!' The patient spat phlegm into a pot he was holding.

'Well anyways,' the whiskered man continued, 'ee'd taken a bad fall from 'ees 'oss at the Meet on Boxing Day. The 'oss came back alone, so Albert said, and there was a right old carry-on at the Big House. 'Es mother was scritching so loud she could be 'eard right down Pipers Pool they d'reckon. An' that Miss Elizabeth were 'aving hysterics, so 'er needed smellin' salts, whatever they be!'

'That there Miss King is a proper spoilt creature, so they d'say.' The other old man nodded, understandingly. 'That maid comes into Lanson town dressed up like a doll... with 'er nose so high in the air tis like 'ers got a pile o' manure under 'en!'

The old men's conversation meandered away from the story of Jasper King's hunting accident, so Kate was no wiser as to the outcome. She made her way out of the room, which seemed too hot suddenly. There was a loud buzzing in her ears and her heart seemed to be beating furiously. What had actually happened to Jasper? Had he been found quickly after his fall? Was he badly injured? Was he dead, even? No, she dismissed the latter idea, feeling sure the news would have travelled quickly of such a tragedy to the wealthy Kings of Tregeare. How could she find out?

Hours later at the end of a long day in the Infirmary, a tired Kate made her way along the road towards the town square where the trap from Werrington would pick her up. She huddled into her warm winter coat with its collar turned up, for the weather was dry but very cold. A few lights from lamps were still shining from windows as men in long white aprons and shop-girls swept up after the day's business. The year was dragging towards its end, old and tired. Soon the New Year would be celebrated and the bells of the churches would ring it in with a spirit of hope.

Was there hope in her own heart, she asked herself? And how was Jasper King after his accident? He had not been brought into the Infirmary with terrible injuries, but that was not a surprise. The Kings had money, so no doubt they had their own physician to attend to their needs at home, in Tregeare House. She could hardly imagine Jasper's handsome face staring out from one of the line of beds in the men's room, wedged between whiskery old men and injured navvies.

Her mind was so crowded with thoughts and unanswered questions that she did not even see Isaac Penhale before she collided with him in the semi-darkness outside the stables of the White Hart.

'Whoa! Steady on,' his friendly voice was easily recognised in the gloaming. He peered closely at her, 'Well if it isn't Miss Polglaze, Jasper's friend from the Werrington estate. What on earth are you doing here alone, in Launceston Square in the near-darkness? You look frozen with the cold.' He noticed her body shaking and her beautiful face as pale as alabaster. 'Perhaps we should call into the White Hart for you to have a hot drink while we have a little talk.'

As the Werrington trap was nowhere to be seen, Kate allowed herself to be shepherded into the warmth and bustle of the coaching inn. She hoped fervently that as luck would have it, she would now be able to find out all about Jasper and his hunting accident from his old school-friend, Isaac Penhale.

Ignoring all the heads turning, meaningful looks and whispers at them both, she sat thankfully by the blazing log fire, sipping the mulled wine the serving-girl gave her.

'I imagine you want to talk about Jasper,' Isaac's expression grew serious. He put his glass down precisely, then looked at Kate, face to face.

'It does not make pleasant listening, I am afraid.'

Chapter 34.

Mary Jane had been ill over Christmas, her mother had been told, confined to her bed in the room up in the rafters of the farmhouse. Old Sarah had stumped her way slowly and breathlessly into Egloskerry and then up the lane to Killicoff with the news. Every now and then she had stopped to think over the words she would use, catching her breath as she did so. She was pleased that none of they navvies were anywhere to be seen, as she pushed open the gate and puffed her way past the pump to the cottage door. What a carry-on it all was, but she was certain in her often confused old mind that it was a navvy behind all this nasty business with Mary Jane, possibly even one of the gang who lived in her family home with her own parents!

Near to collapse, Sarah sat on the settle at Killicoff and drank a welcome dish o'tay with Mrs. Jenkin for her trouble. The two women talked quietly for a while, but Sarah remembered her solemn promise to Mary Jane and made sure she did not 'let the cat out of the bag' as she called it. She assured the anxious, exhausted-looking mother that her daughter was well on the way to recovery. Christmas was all but over, and now it was nearly time to see the old year out, and welcome in the New Year with the secrets it had in store for them all.

Back at Badharlick Mary Jane lay in her narrow bed like a log for days. Her body ached when she moved, but it was her mind that was most affected by the terrible happenings of Christmas Eve. She kept re-living the awful things that had taken place in the darkness on what should have been a Holy night, straight after taking her communion in St. Keri's church. She was riddled with inexplicable feelings of guilt.

It was New Year's Eve before she made her appearance downstairs, ready to do a day's work in the dairy. The Baron family who farmed Badharlick, had been surprisingly understanding about her absence from her tasks. The farmer's wife had commented to old Sarah, the rest of them did not want to pick up any disease that may be lurking in Mary Jane's body. Better for her to make a full recovery in her room up in the rafters, where there would be draughts of fresh air, no doubt, to chase away any sickness. But the girl herself knew well that it would take more n' fresh air to make her feel better...

Mary Jane's cheek still had a greenish bruised look, and her right eye was slightly bloodshot when she came down the back stairs, but apart from that and the fact that she seemed to have lost some weight in only a few days, there she was back out in the dairy scrubbing out pans and churning butter like there was no tomorrow. Only old Sarah knew the heartache she was enduring inside, turning to her work in an effort to blot out the terrible happenings of Christmas Eve.

Late morning a horse's hooves could be heard coming down the hill from Tregeare Green past the farm gates, the iron shoes occasionally slipping with a metallic slurring sound. Sarah was out in the yard scattering corn for the hens when the horse was reined to a standstill by the granite posts and a young man with a pleasant face spoke to her. William Treglown was bidding the old woman a Happy New Year, presuming she would be bringing in the New and saying farewell to the Old that coming night. But it was obvious that he was craning his neck from his horse looking for a glimpse of Mary Jane.

'There won't be much celebrating going on here, sir,' she muttered, unable to look him directly in the eye. 'If you're looking for her, our

Mary Jane has been very unwell over the Christmas and she needs some peace and quiet to recover.'

William's face grew alarmed, but the old woman placated him by saying the maid would soon be back to her usual self. She was simply tired out after her sickness. Looking relieved to hear those words, William asked Sarah to convey his best wishes to Mary Jane and wish her a speedy recovery. Then he clicked his tongue to his mare, which was champing at her bit by then, and rode on down the slope towards the meandering river in the valley below.

In the distance the muted sounds of men at work could be heard, echoing up the valley sides. The bridge at New Mills was being built further down to carry a road over the eventual railway line, and a deep cutting was being excavated somewhere to the south of Egloskerry church. The village gossip was that they were even using dynamite to blast any areas of hard rock! Dynamite, here in their beloved village! Two navvies had sustained serious injuries when blasting before Christmas apparently. Whatever next, was the talk in the Post Office. The women sometimes forgot they had come in to buy a pinch of pepper, or post a small parcel or buy a solitary stamp for a letter, often written for them by the vicar or the local schoolteacher; they would gather in twos or threes, whispering over the latest happenings, wondering what the next piece of sacrilege would be on their green and pleasant land.

Old Sarah sighed deeply as she turned back towards the farmhouse. She could hear the rhythmic skirring sound of the butter churn being turned, out in the dairy by Mary Jane. Poor maid, she thought as she peeped in at her, unseen. She seemed to have lost her fresh, innocent look over the past few days for her face was so pale and her normally glorious hair, straggling untidily from below her cap, looked lank and lifeless. And no wonder! At times old Sarah truly believed the Devil himself must be at work here in their midst.

'Is the butter coming then Mary Jane?' Sarah's voice made the girl start, as she had been mechanically turning the wooden handle in something of a daze.

'Oh tis you Sarah, you made my heart jump!' She let go of the handle and put her shaking hand up to her mouth.

Sarah brushed past her and took hold of the handle, and soon the churning began once more.

For a few minutes there was silence, apart from the rhythmic churning and a distant cockerel crowing to the world.

'I seed that William Treglown of yours out be the gate on 'ees 'oss a while back,' Sarah spoke quietly, but did not look up from her relentless churning.

'He's not my William Treglown no more,' Mary Jane's quiet voice trembled as she spoke. 'He never was, if the truth is known. But now tis best that he keeps away from Badharlick... and from me. For I'm not the same maid I was afore Christmas.' Her voice tailed off into nothing.

The handle gave a protesting squeak as Sarah suddenly let go her hold on it. 'Now you just listen to me Mary Jane Jenkin! What happened to you on that night was terrible, maid! But you'm strong.' The old woman searched desperately for words. 'You've got to put it out of yer mind, and carry on. That William of yours seems like a good young man to me, you mustn't tell 'im what happened. 'Tis our secret. 'Twill all pass.'

She looked at the girl before her, the tears welling up in her eyes.

'Afore you d'knaw it, the summer'll be here, an' then we'll all be feelin' brighter!'

Mary Jane did not look convinced.

'Now wipe yer eyes on yer apron maid, an' let's get this ere butter churned, afore there's trouble.'

Soon the sound of churning resumed and nothing more was said in the dairy.

Chapter 35.

The month of January was a dreary one, heavy rain, flooded pastures and swollen rivers were the landscape. The work on the railway embankments was held up as a result, for the earth was loosened by the deluge of water and it was considered liable to collapse, hence too dangerous for the workmen. As it was, a young man had been severely injured over at the hamlet of Splatt a few miles from Egloskerry, when he had been running with a horse and he had slipped in the wet muck. The wheels of the wagon which the horse was pulling 'had passed over his bowels', it was later reported in the local newspaper. He had immediately been taken to Doctor Gibson in Launceston, who had tended to his horrific injuries, but simply could not save him. The young man, name of Josiah, had died within hours of the tragic accident.

'What a waste of a young life,' sighed the vicar of Egloskerry, sitting at his writing desk in his cold, damp mausoleum of a vicarage. Outside his window the rain lashed down in the wet, wintry garden, making him think fleetingly of Noah and the Great Flood. His faithful dog looked up at him hopefully, perhaps for scraps which were not often forthcoming from the frugal vicarage table.

The rain continued for what seemed like weeks, and then February brought drying winds and low temperatures. The navvies were all hard at work once more, some using dynamite in areas where the rock was hard. Down in the river-side meadows where Mary Jane used to check on the heifers, the land had been marked out in preparation for the building of the railway station. The gossip was that it would not be built out of local stone, another fact to cause umbrage to the villagers of

Egloskerry. Instead, vast quantities of red bricks would be brought in from some far-off place. It was even said that the Duke of Bedford himself had donated the huge amount of one hundred pounds towards the proposed station!

In the Simcoe Arms, these snippets of news kept the conversation going for the old men over their ale and cider.

'Well the Duke of Bedford be one o' the richest men in England, so they d'say!' An old fellow sitting in the settle by the fire spoke and nodded sagely.

'Ow do 'ee knaw that then Jack?' asked a dumpy man with apple cheeks, ripe enough to be made into scrumpy.

The old fellow took his clay pipe out of his sunken mouth and waved it about a bit for effect. 'My feyther used to be a woodsman for the Duke t'other side o' t Tamar! Sed 'ee 'ad so much money 'ee used t' keep some o' it in a golden teapot on 'is mahogany sideboard!'

The dumpy man's eyes shone like carriage lamps. 'Just think o' that, a teapot made out o' real gold!'

'The tay don't taste no different,' the clay pipe was brandished once more, 'whether 'tis from a gold teapot or an old cracked brown one, like what we got back home.'

'I allus thought the Duke lived at Werrington Park,' Apple-cheeks mused quietly.

'That was another Duke! You'm a proper old fool... That was the Duke of Northumberland.' The clay pipe stabbed the air indignantly as old Jack made his point.

A brief pause was followed by, 'Oh I d' knaw... That there public house in St. Stephen's-by-Lanson is called the Northumberland Arms. Opposite the church. Us often used to call in there, on our way 'ome from market.'

The old men huddled closer to the fire and the conversation soon meandered back to the building of the railway and how it was destroying the good pasture-land surrounding Egloskerry.

Meanwhile over at the previously-mentioned Werrington, Kate Polglaze was mechanically helping her aunt with the daily chores on the farm. In her mind, always very much to the fore, was the news she had received in the White Hart from Isaac Penhale just before the coming of the New Year.

'Jasper was eventually found after his hunter came back to Tregeare House, riderless, with its stirrups flying. It took hours of looking mind you, all the men and boys on the estate were out searching for him. I was there too, as I'd also been out with the hunt that day.' Isaac took a mouthful of his drink and wiped his mouth before he carried on with his tale. 'As the light was beginning to fade, a young lad who works in the stables gave a shout. He'd found the young master, lying in a ditch behind a stone hedge as if he'd had a fall.'

Isaac's voice had gone quiet, so Kate had pressed him gently to continue.

'First of all, we all thought he was dead. He was so white and pale and we could not see him breathing for it was that shallow.' He stopped again, the memory coming fast now. 'He had a great bone sticking out of his leg, horrible it was.' Isaac shuddered. 'The flesh was ragged and torn, he'd lost a lot of blood. Somehow we managed to get him on a hurdle to carry him the miles back to Tregeare, but by then he was groaning like a madman.'

Kate envisaged the scene, knew from her experience in the Infirmary how much pain Jasper must have endured, being jolted across the fields all those miles in the encroaching darkness.

'Both his mother and his sister Elizabeth were nigh-on hysterical when we arrived at their house at Tregeare, and he was carried into the Library and laid on their long table while someone rode for the family doctor.' Isaac had stopped once more, remembering how Philip King, white around the gills, had cleared his shrieking, sobbing women from the room.

'Jasper's father brought in their old children's nurse who had an unflustered, calm way with her. She tended to Jasper as best she could, cutting away his blood-soaked clothes and bathing the terrible wound, until eventually we heard the doctor arrive on horseback, after what had seemed like bloody hours. He administered morphine, and Jasper gradually stopped his awful groaning and became quieter...'

Kate had watched Isaac's expressions as he unfolded the story of the following hours: the awful sound of the bone being manipulated back into place, Jasper's screams of agony, the father biting his lip as he watched his eldest son and heir going through some kind of hell on earth.

Isaac told how Philip King had poured out large brandies for them both in his study, confiding in his son's friend. It was all spoilt now, for sure his son would never be the same again. The important thing was that his son should survive, come through this accident and not lose his leg. As the brandy worked on the emotional father, he had described the argument he'd had with Jasper only the night before the hunt. He admitted he was feeling somewhat responsible for his son's frame of mind...

After consuming more brandy with Isaac so that his speech was slurred, Philip King had convinced himself he was a tyrant. He was drunk, morose. What did it really matter if Jasper didn't make a good match to an heiress? Was it really so awful that he had fallen in love with some chit of a girl from a farm out at Werrington? Better than his son dying... when all was said and done.

Here Kate, who had been listening to this tale of near tragedy from Isaac Penhale, had reacted at last. Up till then she had remained calm on the outside, but then she'd taken in a deep breath and all her own senses had tingled.

Being described as 'some chit of a girl' would normally have made her blood boil! How cheap it made her sound! Yet these were the rambling words of Philip King, distraught at his son Jasper's hunting accident and drunk as a Lord. Isaac was also clearly distressed about the condition of his friend, getting emotional as he had told Kate the whole story, just before the New Year had bade its farewell to the Old.

Miserable weeks had passed slowly since then, with no word of Jasper's condition. All Kate knew was that he had not been brought into the Infirmary at Launceston, so he must be receiving treatment and care at home. She was increasingly determined that she would see him face-to-face, before very much longer, even if that meant making her own way out to Tregeare House and standing like a veritable post outside his door! The more she thought about it, the more the plan began to take root and grow in her mind.

So it was on a cold day in late February that Kate Polglaze could be seen warmly wrapped up in the Werrington trap bowling along the road to Egloskerry and down past Well Meadow towards the river at the bottom of the valley. The pony strained on the uphill climb past Badharlick towards the hamlet of Tregeare, so Kate alighted to walk up the slope, to lessen the pony's load.

As she passed the gates of the farmhouse at Badharlick, she caught a fleeting glimpse of a young woman's pale face surrounded by a mass of red-gold hair at the window. Their eyes locked momentarily and then the face at the window quickly disappeared from view.

Two country girls, unknown to each other, both with their hearts and minds captured by young men who lived in the nearby parish of Tregeare.

The pony and trap continued steadily on its way, before long emerging onto the high ground of Tregeare Down, before dipping down through an avenue of ancient oak trees.

At last Kate had arrived at the tranquil hamlet of Tregeare with its village green. She could see a pretty cottage next to a gateway, with a sign saying North Lodge. Ahead of her, was a long winding drive which must be the entrance to Tregeare House, as yet hidden from view by the trees.

Her heart seemed to beat more quickly as the pony and trap moved towards its destination and her mind was full of doubts and confusion. What was she thinking of, coming all the way out here, on her own? She should have persuaded Jasper's friend, Isaac Penhale, to accompany her at the very least.

But as the trap proceeded through the trees round a corner of the drive, the sight of the elegant Italianate house stunned her. It quite simply took her breath away. This was a house for the really rich, for gentlemen such as Philip King, and sons like Jasper. Kate pulled on the pony's reins and the trap, little more than a painted cart, paused on the drive-way; she sat with the reins held loosely in her hands, feeling lost and foolish.

How on the Lord's earth had she ever thought she could be connected in a romantic way to a young man from such a family, living in something so magnificent?

Chapter 36.

Kate climbed down from the trap in front of the dazzling white house with its pillars and classical appearance, feeling severely out of place in her drab clothes which were travel-stained from the journey. The clothes had not seemed drab when she had dressed by candle-light in the early morning at her aunt's at Werrington, but now she felt distinctly shabby, for even her hair was tumbling down wildly from its pins.

A weathered-looking man in a worn leather apron appeared around the corner, from the hidden stables. He did not look at all surprised to see an unaccompanied young woman, standing next to a trap with a tired-looking pony between its shafts. He touched his forelock as if she was the Queen of Sheba and led the pony and trap away behind the house to the stable-yard, where the Kings stabled their glossy, thorough-bred horses, no doubt. The sound of the pony's hoofs on the cobbles faded away and Kate stood alone, facing the main entrance doors at the front of the house. Behind her were the sweeping lawns and Bodmin Moor in the distance.

She looked up at the upstairs twelve-pane sash windows, wondering if one of them could be Jasper's bedroom. Was he even now lying in there, tended by his anxious mother? As she gazed upwards, she thought she saw a curtain being pulled aside, as if there was a watcher there.

Kate smoothed her wayward hair and straightened her shoulders before ascending the few steps to the double front door between the pillars. Her heart was hammering away as she tugged the elegant bell-pull. She could hear it echo inside the hallway. A brief pause, then a neatly-dressed housemaid opened the door.

'I have come to see Mr. King if that is possible...' Kate's voice did not sound at all like her own as she blurted out the words. She cleared her throat nervously.

The housemaid, Rosie, took it all in at a glance; the rather dishevelled-looking young woman in plain clothes, but what an abundance of black hair and such a beautiful face!

'Mr. King is not here I am afraid. He is away on business in Plymouth,' Rosie's voice was apologetic.

'Oh no,' Kate spoke more loudly. 'I mean... Mr. Jasper King. The son of... your master.' She boldly continued, 'I believe he had a hunting accident straight after Christmas. Well so his friend Mr. Isaac Penhale told me.' There was a pause. 'I have come a long way and I would like to see him, if that is at all possible.'

Rosie looked distinctly uncomfortable. She did not like to ask this unknown young woman into the house, yet she felt sympathy for her.

'Who is it Rosie?' The sharp, yet familiar voice of Elizabeth King echoed through the hallway.

'It's a ... young lady Miss Elizabeth. To see Master Jasper.' Rosie's voice faltered, as if she knew she would pay for this later. She stood back to one side, as if trying to make herself invisible.

Elizabeth appeared at the bottom of the staircase, looking immaculate as ever in a cherry-coloured day dress with a paisley shawl draped around her shoulders.

'Surely it's not Miss Polglaze?' Elizabeth's tone was incredulous. 'All the way out here at Tregeare?'

Kate flushed with embarrassment. She could see the maidservant standing as still as one of the pillars, listening attentively. No doubt this meeting would soon be all re-told in the domestic quarters behind the green baize covered door.

'Yes it is, it's Kate Polglaze. I've come all the way from Werrington. Good day to you Miss King.' This was the one person she did not wish to meet at Tregeare House. However she ran her tongue over her dry lips and murmured, 'I came to enquire how your brother Jasper is, after his unfortunate accident during the hunt.'

'Well this is most unusual.' Elizabeth still had not invited Kate into the hall-way of the house. Rosie listened and watched, as Elizabeth continued, her voice cold and clipped. 'My brother has been through the most terrible time since Boxing Day.' Elizabeth paused and looked straight at Kate, shivering visibly on the doorstep. 'And he won't be expecting you of course.'

Rosie coughed suddenly, trying desperately to muffle it in her apron. Elizabeth whipped round on her like a snake. 'That will be all Rosie!'

The girl bobbed a curtsey and disappeared quickly behind the green baize door. As the door closed tightly behind her, Rosie muttered to herself under her breath, 'What a cold-hearted bitch that woman is.'

Kate drew herself up to her full height and forced herself to smile brightly at Jasper's sister. 'I know for certain that he will want to see me, Elizabeth! His good friend Isaac Penhale has been talking to me about the hunting accident and how frustrated Jasper is to be shut away from the world while he recuperates.'

At the mention of Isaac Penhale's name, the future baronet, Elizabeth's marble-white cheeks coloured a little.

Suddenly, the double doors to the Library swung open and Anne King, Elizabeth's mother, emerged frowning.

'What on earth is going on out here Elizabeth? It is freezing in the hall with the front doors wide open!' She stopped on seeing the woman, a stranger, standing outside on the doorstep.

'This is Miss Kate Polglaze mother,' her daughter's voice was heavy with meaning.

There was a slight pause while Anne King took this in, before she spoke. This then was the penniless woman who her son had supposedly fallen in love with, and who had ruined the end of their family Christmas Day.

'For goodness sake,' Anne's voice was irritable, 'Ask the young woman to step inside, into the warmth of the house. Where are your manners Elizabeth?'

Kate stepped gratefully into the hallway, noting in a glance the long row of staff bells just inside the door and the archway leading to the graceful staircase within.

An exasperated voice, Jasper's, shouted from the depths of the Library, 'Mother? What the devil is going on out there?'

Kate kept calm and waited, but the petulant voice made her smile.

In a blur she was ushered without more ado into the Library by the mother, Anne King. There in front of the blazing log-fire with his back to her, lay Jasper on an elegant chaise-longue and with his injured leg resting on a pile of cushions. He craned his neck a little to see who it was, standing behind him.

'Well come in then whoever you are!' His voice sounded like a man truly out-of-sorts. 'Don't just stand there where I can't see you!'

In a sudden rustle of skirts, his mother faced her son, while Kate did not move a muscle waiting to be introduced.

'It is an acquaintance of yours, Jasper... a Miss Polglaze, come all the way from the Werrington estate.' Her tone was somewhat acid.

'Come in Miss Polglaze and warm yourself near the fire!'

Kate had never seen Jasper so still and silent. It was as if the power of speech had simply deserted him. As she came around from behind the chaise-longue towards the fire so that he could actually see her in the flesh, he sat bolt upright, wrenching his injured leg, and then gasped out her name, 'Kate?'

'Hello Jasper.' Her voice was husky, yet gentle towards him. 'Isaac Penhale has been telling me how you have been suffering after your accident.' She paused, aware of Elizabeth in the background watching her through hooded eyes, like some kind of predatory hawk. 'So I plucked up the courage to come and see how you are recuperating for myself.'

'Kate… I can't believe you have made the journey all those miles out here to see me,' Jasper's eyes were fixed on hers, as if there was no-one else in the room.

Anne King was only too aware of the wordless exchange between the two of them, so she broke the tension with the calming words, 'Please sit down Miss Polglaze while I ring for some refreshments.' Then she continued, 'No doubt you will be glad of a hot drink… before your return journey.'

'That will be much appreciated, Mrs. King.'

Kate perched, her back ram-rod straight, on the edge of an elegant fireside chair. Jasper glared across at his mother, who he usually adored, as she pulled the bell-sash. It was obvious she wanted rid of Kate as soon as was possible.

It seemed forever before Rosie appeared at the double doors, bobbing her little curtsey to her mistress. Meanwhile conversation was stilted in the Library, although all seemed polite on the surface.

Still Jasper could not take his eyes off Kate, he could not believe this lovely young woman had risked censure from his family to come to see him. Yes, her appearance proved to him that not only was she beautiful in a dark exotic way, but she was brave with it! She had done nothing to encourage him, but he knew then that he would not give her up.

'Did you come in the Werrington Park carriage?' Elizabeth asked maliciously, her eyes gleaming.

Kate realized that it was probably Elizabeth herself who had pulled back the upstairs curtain, watching her arrival.

'No Elizabeth!' Kate's eyes sparkled at the obvious attempt at humiliation. 'I drove myself out here in the pony and trap. I do so love to be out in the fresh air, in the countryside, even though it is extremely cold today... but then, it is still only late February.' She would have loved to make a comment about the good old country smell of cow shit, like she had on their very first meeting when she had clashed with Miss High-and-Mighty Elizabeth King.

'How very modern of you Miss Polglaze,' driving yourself around the back lanes with no chaperone!' Anne King spoke quietly, but there was obvious disapproval in her tone.

The tray of tea arrived and so conversation lulled while bone-china cups were filled and a dainty plate of newly-baked biscuits was passed around.

Jasper motioned Kate to a chair nearer to him, so that they could talk more easily. At first she hesitated, looking at his mother for some sort of guidance, but she was reprimanding Rosie for some little thing or other, so Kate moved slightly closer and at last Jasper started to tell her his version of his accident and the long, arduous recovery.

'I suppose you are used to this sort of thing, working as you do in the Infirmary till all hours,' Elizabeth could not resist chipping in. 'We have our own family doctor of course, here at Tregeare House, and he has been dealing with Jasper's injuries. No common sick-bed in the Infirmary for my brother!' She smiled at Kate with barely concealed venom.

'I would expect nothing less for someone like Jasper,' Kate spoke softly, wondering just how a girl like Elizabeth could be so full of spite. 'Yet there are amazing things done for the patients in the Infirmary nowadays, and the study of medicine is improving all the time!'

'Well said Kate!' Jasper applauded loudly, catching the attention of his mother who quickly banished poor Rosie to the kitchens and returned to the fireside. She realized she had neglected to keep an eye on her son and this enigmatic girl from Werrington, who appeared to have eyes only for each other. At least she was not clinging on to him, but for all that, it was probably time she left.

'I am sure Miss Polglaze will need to leave soon, for she has an arduous journey before her, and on her own too,' Anne smiled politely, always the perfect hostess. 'It is so kind of you to visit my son Jasper like this… even if it was unexpected!'

Elizabeth smirked behind her mother's back.

Of course. A lady would not even dream of doing such a thing. Kate stood up hastily and a tangled black ringlet fell from its pins as she did so. Jasper was mesmerized, watching it tumble down onto her breast, as he looked up at her from the chaise-longue.

The room became silent as Kate prepared to take her leave. The pony and trap had been hastily ordered from the stables. As she pulled on her leather gloves, she thought to herself that her visit had not been as terrible as she had expected. She had seen Jasper, which is all that she had wanted. He was very much alive and recovering from his injuries. She had braved his family and if anything made them feel uncomfortable, rather than herself!

As Kate was seen out of the door by an increasingly flustered-looking Rosie, Jasper sat bright-eyed, staring into the flames.

He knew without any doubt that this was the woman he wanted, intended to marry even. It did not matter to him one bit that she was not of their class! But Jasper was realistic. He knew also that there would be nothing but confrontation with his father to face in the days ahead.

Chapter 37.

Mary Jane had seen the pony and trap passing up the hill towards Tregeare earlier in the day, from the farmhouse window at Badharlick. She also heard it returning, past the farmyard gates, in the afternoon. She had been round the back, in the privvy, feeling unwell. She had felt nauseous these past few days and had even vomited near the vegetable garden the day before, wondering what she had eaten to make her feel so vile. As she emerged, she picked up a bucket of scraps for the fowls and came around the corner of the farmhouse; she saw the trap with the same unknown woman, holding the reins tightly in her gloved hands. Wherever she had been and what she had been doing since the morning, was unknown. But Mary Jane saw the young woman's lovely face looked troubled and the mass of black hair was now looking wild and unkempt. She could not help but wonder who she was.

Kate on the other hand, glanced quickly to her left towards the farmhouse where she had seen a pale face at the window framed by red-gold hair. She saw what looked like a milkmaid coming around the corner, her face deathly-pale, the bright hair partly hidden under a cap. Their eyes met briefly for the second time that day. Kate gave a barely perceptible nod towards her, as if her mind was elsewhere, before the pony continued down the hill towards the river at the bottom and she was soon out of sight.

As the February afternoon wore on, it became bitterly cold. Down in the Kensey valley working on the railway, men and boys blew on their frozen fingers and longed for the warmer days ahead. Work was tough when they worked in the grim shadow of Red Down, or Riddon as the locals called it, and before long the darkness began to creep in so it was down tools for the day. They started to troop homewards, grey dirt-covered figures in the gloom, their voices echoing along the valley sides.

At Badharlick in the farmhouse kitchen a huge fire was burning in the cavernous fireplace. If you sat next to it, in one of the tall settles, you would roast. If you were further away in the draught from the door, your teeth would soon chatter with the cold. That evening a handful of the farm servants were toasting themselves, hands held out to the leaping flames. The farmer and his wife were enjoying the privacy of their own living room, with its comfortable armchairs, warm rugs and other trappings, a cat sleeping peacefully on the hearth in front of the glowing log fire.

In the kitchen the servants were having a yarn about the building of the railway as usual, and various other bits of gossip that had been passed on from the Simcoe Arms in Egloskerry, like who was thought to have 'rinned off' with whom. One recent story from Launceston was that the landlord of the Railway Inn had been violently attacked by seven men, when out for a ride on his horse. It went without saying that the farm labourers blamed this loudly and vocally on the navvies, who gathered together in gangs in the nearby market town. After all, they were reknown as drunken criminals when all was said and done. You only had to read the local newspaper (that's if you could read it for yourself, or get someone else to read it all out for you) to find out about the navvies' poaching and their other criminal actions.

Old Sarah sat nearest to the fireplace, her tough old skin like leather seeming to withstand the intense heat. She was quiet for once, brooding over something or other, her gnarled hands folded on her voluminous apron. Mary Jane was sitting back in the shadows, looking pale and ghostly in comparison to the ruddy faces of the work-men, basking in the heat.

'Tes no good, I'm sweating like a pig!' One of the men, Jan Higgins wiped his brow and drained his last dregs of cider, before standing up with much creaking of his bones. 'I'm better out in the barns, doin' me last check on the beasts than in 'ere, roasting me own flesh! I'll bid ee all good night neighbours,' so saying he squashed his felt hat onto his head and opened the door, a blast of cold air entering the room. The remaining two labourers looked at each other and got up, draining their last drops, following one after the other as if they were cows going into the yard for milking.

The kitchen seemed strangely quiet after the deep voices of the menfolk. Mary Jane picked up their mugs and put them near the slate sink for rinsing. Sarah watched the girl from beneath tired, hooded eyes.

'You'm looking some whisht and pale, Mary Jane. Be 'ee sure you be feelin' proper maid?'

The girl nodded, with her back rigidly towards Sarah as she stood at the sink.

There was a moment of silence, broken only by the shifting of a log on the fire.

Sarah tried again to rouse Mary Jane into some sort of life. 'I seed William Treglown today passing the farm. He was asking fer 'ee. Said ee'd not seen a hair of your head, maid, for weeks now.'

There was no reply from the sink, just a loud clattering as Mane Jane rinsed off some plates, crashing them against the slate sides.

'Mary Jane?' The old woman persisted.

The girl spun round, her red hair lit by the firelight so that she looked like some fierce maenad. 'Stop going on at me day after day about William Treglown, Sarah! I can't see him and let that be an end to it all!' Her eyes glittered with pent-up angry tears.

Sarah was shocked by her outburst. She knew things were not right for the maid, but Mary Jane had never shouted at her like this before! It quite took her breath away. Her poor old heart was fair hammering in her ample bosom, like one of they big drums they played at the Egloskerry Fair each summer.

In the light of the fire Sarah could see the tears glittering in the girl's eyes, ready to spill over.

'Tes all ruined,' Mary Jane's voice shook. 'I am sick in my stomach every day, from the first moment I wake up. I can't eat proper, so tisn't anything I have ate. I just keep being sick...'

Old Sarah was even more shocked as she struggled to understand what Mary Jane was telling her.

'I can't bear to think of it,' the tears began to well over and fall, shining in the firelight, 'but I'm a-feared that I have a baby growing in my belly.'

'My dear Lord,' Sarah's voice came out a husky whisper. 'No wonder you'm all out o' sorts maid.' She stopped to think, her poor old mind quite befuddled. 'Be 'ee sure 'bout it Mary Jane? Sometimes these feelings be all wrong.'

Mary Jane came over to the old woman and sat down shakily on the settle, twisting her apron in her work-reddened hands.

'Now you d'know why I can't bear you to talk of William nigh on every day.' Her voice was so low it could hardly be heard. 'That were all a dream, an innocent sweet dream of last summer.'

She dashed away the tears with her hand, for Mary Jane had to be strong now. What in the world would her parents say to this most terrible happening? Her father would be angry, violent even. He would put pressure on her to marry the man no doubt, not that she even knew who he was! She knew only too well about other girls in the village who had gotten into trouble, and how they were stared at and ostracized by some of the women, even those holier-than-thou chapel and church goers who should have been more charitable. She knew also that a servant getting with child could mean instant dismissal, so that many girls and young women concealed their pregnancy until the last possible moment, and who could blame them? She had even heard of new-born babies being found abandoned, smothered, or even strangled. Babies left in a ditch to die…

Sarah reached out her gnarled, bent old hands and took hold of Mary Jane's shaking ones.

'Now you just listen to me, maid. Tis our secret fer now, no-one else needs t'know.' She squeezed her hands comfortingly. 'An' we'll sort out what's going to happen... dreckly.'

Chapter 38.

The navvies were reknown as drinkers. Everyone knew that, before they ever arrived in Egloskerry and the surrounding area. So they had settled in nicely in the Simcoe Arms, spending copious amounts of hard-earned money on ale. At first the landlord had rubbed his hands together at the thought of his fat profits. However, he had not reckoned with the fact that the navvies simply liked fighting! If they didn't fight with any locals who were stupid enough to stand up to them, then they would fight with each other. The vicar of Egloskerry was driven to distraction with the complaints of his parishioners.

The Police in nearby Launceston had been given early warning before their arrival to North Cornwall to be 'constantly on the alert' in their newly-built Police Station in Launceston; the magistrates had been notified from on high that they too must be prepared to deal severely with these gangs of lawless railway workers. Who knew, even the Riot Act might need to be read in the town Square!

The month of March blew in on its crazy, wild winds and somehow it did something to these men, who liked nothing better than to swagger and show off. So it was that on one Friday night in the Simcoe Arms, the public house was crammed with over-exuberant navvies, money in their pockets, swilling ale at a great rate of knots to slake the thirst they had worked up earlier that day. The heat and the noise was insufferable, so the few old men who drank cider quietly in a dark corner, tottered off home, fearing something was about to blow.

Among these navvies in the Simcoe Arms that night was the tough bunch of men lodging up the lane in the three cottages which made up Killicoff. This was of course the family home of Mary Jane Jenkin, whose father had been tempted by the glint of gold in his usually mundane life of trying to eke out a poor existence from the few acres of land he rented to support his growing family.

Further along the lane in the three cottages at Trebeath there were another thirteen navvies lodging, and most of them had walked down to Egloskerry that evening to sup as much beer as possible. So with the addition of a couple of beefy plate-layers lodging in the hamlet of Badharlick, the inn was well and truly packed out that night. Beer and navvies, an explosive mix!

The landlord's wife was a buxom woman, perspiring so much she was as red in the face as shiny tomato, with large heaving breasts which strained against her tightly-laced bodice. She was serving pint pots of ale as fast as she could, squeezed behind the bar which was greasy with the elbows and coats of all the customers. More than a few lewd comments were shouted about her by the younger men who were rapidly getting drunk, showing off to each other about their own prowess at sleeping with women, young and old. Even a fat old woman like the landlady! They'd show her a good time! A bright spark shouted they could even share her around! Roars of laughter camouflaged this, so that the landlord heard only a general hubbub of voices. It was as if he was under water, for he was sure he was going deaf like his father before him, which was probably just as well on this occasion.

The boasting grew, so that before long some of the younger men (who were not as practised at holding their ale), were spilling out embellished stories on all their recent acts of outrage, some back as far as last summer. They relished being in the midst of their own kind, tough and often ruthless men who had travelled the length of the land building canals and bridges, using explosives to cut through resistant rock-face, before the laying of endless miles of track for the railway.

One small group of younger men clustered near the open door of the public house, getting steadily more and more inebriated as the evening wore on. One of them did not have the usual navvies' muscles, he was thin and elongated, with a somewhat weasely appearance. He and his mates had now got on to drinking gin and its effects were beginning to show.

'Do ye remember that robbery last spring, over at the farm near the chapel? That were right good!' His bony face lit up at the thought.

Another laughed loudly at the vague memory. 'If you mean over at Athill, it were that easy. Just a simple farmer's boy on his way whoam from market. It were like takin' a titty bottle off a babby!'

The first man, the weasel, continued, 'You all gave 'im a right good kicking after. That showed him... ' He slurred, 'Don't suppose that there lass wi' the golden hair looked at 'im after...' He took a slug of brandy and wiped his wet mouth.

'Which lass wi' the golden hair?' a good-looking young man as dark as a gypsy and with contrasting white teeth scowled across at The Weasel. 'You don't mean the lass of old man Jenkin, from our lodgings at Killicoff? What 's she got to do wi' it?'

'They do say the lass was fond o' him... The farmer's boy you all left bleedin' int' ditch, at Athill or whativer it's called.' The Weasel took another slug at his brandy.

The three others looked at each other in amazement before closing in menacingly on The Weasel. 'What do you mean, YOU all left at Athill. You were there too, supposedly keepin' watch as always.' One particularly muscular navvy grabbed hold of his collar roughly and shook him like a rag doll.

'We ALL left him in t' ditch, if I d'remember. But then you don't have neither the guts nor the muscles to actually fight.' He let go of The Weasel's collar in disgust.

'But you were bloody quick to go through his pockets and take his money-bag!' snarled the man who had the look of a gypsy, spitting with venom on the sanded floor.

The Weasel attempted to pull himself together, 'Come on lads!' He spoke weakly, almost pleading. 'We're all in this together.' He moved away slightly, looking suddenly nervous. 'Let me buy us all some gin. That'll put us right...' He sidled off towards the bar, squeezing his spare frame amongst the heaving crowd, making a quick exit before tempers got more frayed and they all came to blows.

Outside the door of the Simcoe Arms, young Sam, a village boy, loitered in the shadows. He had heard the younger navvies talking, heard them laughing about their attack on William Treglown nigh on a year before, before robbing him of his money from the market. He slunk into the deeper shadows, ducking down on his haunches behind the garden wall of Church Cottage. What should he do? His heart was pounding, for those men were violent and his life wouldn't be worth living if they found out that they'd been overheard! He picked at an irritating spot on his cheek and made it bleed while he thought. Old Mrs. Gynn would have been abed hours ago in the tiny cottage, so Sam decided to stay put, hiding inside her garden wall for a while longer. Just to be on the safe side.

Meanwhile inside the public house, the temperature had risen and so had men's hot tempers. It was not long before a fight broke out and spilled out into the lane outside. Shouting and swearing, the navvies went hammer and tongs at each other, until lips were split, eyes were blackened and shirts torn. It was getting late, and the landlord had watched his public house empty before his very eyes. He took quick advantage of it and bolted the doors securely for the night. No amount of hammering would induce him to open the doors again that night.

Outside, the brawling continued until men grew tired, swaying on their feet. They could not even remember what they had been fighting about! Some had drifted off, to their wives and a couple to their women who they had married over the broomstick. The younger ones slouched against the walls of the Simcoe Arms, smoking and swearing loudly, so that many a curtain twitched in the surrounding cottages. But no-one dared to shout at them to stop their yelling and get off back to their lodgings. The navvies were outsiders and would probably all roast in Hell when it came down to it!

One man walked up the lane alone towards Penheale Lodge. He was as dark as a gypsy, his eyes shining like little stars. He needed time to think. To think about the girl with the red-gold hair, the girl he had attacked after church while drunk on Christmas Eve. What had he actually done to her? It was all a blur. But earlier tonight in the Simcoe Arms the same pretty farm girl, daughter of his landlord at Killicoff so-to-speak, had come into the conversation; then he'd discovered that the man they'd attacked and left for dead in a ditch at Little Athill was said to have been her young man. My God what a bloody mess... he was getting as bad as his hated father, who had got so drunk on one occasion that he had sold his woman for a gallon of beer!

But one thing he did remember. He had heard how a navvy up country somewhere had been convicted of some outrage, maybe a robbery or worse, and hanged by the side of the railway line as a warning to his wayward work-mates.

He spat into the hedge. There was a rustling as if some small wild creature had been disturbed.

Perhaps it was time he moved on. Pick up his few belongings from his lodgings at Killicoff and leave tonight. He was sick of it anyway.

He spat once more, a bitter taste in his mouth. The railway line from Launceston to Egloskerry would have to be bloody well finished without him.

Chapter 39.

The days stretched into weeks. Kate Polglaze looked back on her impromptu visit to Tregeare House and wondered at her own courage, or had it been sheer madness on her part? She went about her daily tasks on the farm at Werrington, while her aunt sat with a vacant look on her face. Aunt Nell had lost her busy little ways, feeding the hens, scalding the cream, baking bread and making pasties. She was now as monosyllabic as her son, Kate's cousin Jack, only speaking when she was spoken to. Jack continued to wolf back huge amounts of food, work till the light faded and then snore in his father's chair in the kitchen. So Kate had plenty of time to think and ponder. Life was safe, but dull.

Then there was her work in the Infirmary, which was hard graft but still rewarding in its own way. The injured navvy, Thomas Martock, had gone home at last. He'd shed a few tears when he said his goodbyes, especially to 'his Angel' Kate, who had given him gentle support since his terrible accident in the explosion many months before. His sight had returned a little, and he had regained some of his former strength. His tired-looking mother had made the long journey down on the train to Launceston to take him back home. But they both knew that he would never be the same man again. His empty coat sleeve was pinned up neatly to his shoulder as a harsh visible reminder that his life as a navvy, building the railways, was well and truly over.

As Kate rolled what seemed like miles of bandages, her mind often dwelt on Jasper and wondered how he was making his recovery. She had gone back to their meeting at Tregeare House over and over in her mind: his surprise and delight at seeing her, his dark eyes following her around the room as if afraid she might disappear once more. The way he had praised her for her words about the Infirmary and the advances in medicine, despite his sister Elizabeth's caustic remarks; the way he had watched, as if fascinated, as her hair had tumbled down on her breast...

Then one morning Kate heard a voice she thought she recognized, echoing loudly out in the hospital entrance. It was that of Philip King, Jasper's father. She took a deep breath, wondering what had brought him to visit the Infirmary, but then she remembered hearing that he was on the Board, one of the Infirmary's wealthier benefactors. No doubt the doctor would be fawning over him before too long!

She returned to her tasks, tending to an old man who lay in pain and confusion wondering just where he was. She spoke to him gently, smoothed his feverish brow, unknowing that Philip King had entered the room with the stiffly starched nurse who had given Jasper so much grief on his brief visit months before. He was quietly observing the scene.

'And this is our Voluntary nurse, Mr. King. Miss Katherine Polglaze.'

Kate swivelled to face Jasper's father. The man who had referred to her as 'some chit of a girl from a farm out at Werrington,' according to Isaac Penhale. Her face was calm as she greeted him politely, hiding any of her true feelings behind a mask.

His eyes raked over her, noting the fine dark eyes and the curve of her mouth. If anything, the white uniform and headscarf covering most of her luxuriant black hair accentuated her natural beauty. This, then, was the young woman his son was supposedly in love with. He had been prepared to dislike the girl immediately, but there was something about her... he felt caught by her intoxicating appearance. No wonder Jasper had been making such a bloody fool of himself! If he were a few years younger he would probably have been making her into one of his secret mistresses! But for his son to marry her... surely it was unthinkable.

'Miss Polglaze.' His voice was stony, putting distance between them.

'Mr. King.' Kate risked the mere shadow of a smile, disarming him somewhat.

The starched nurse's attention was caught by a patient and she stalked over to a sick-bed at the far end of the room. Philip King was the one who felt suddenly uncomfortable. This girl's coolness in her nun-like attire seemed to undermine him.

He cleared his throat and spoke again, hardly believing what he was saying. 'I believe I must thank you for visiting my son Jasper after his accident. My dear wife told me you had called at Tregeare House.' There was a brief silence, then he added as an afterthought, 'And my daughter Elizabeth, of course.'

Kate could well imagine how Elizabeth had described the uninvited visit; yet she smiled at this man with a face like Cornish granite and said in her smooth voice, 'It was a pleasure to see that Jasper is making such a good recovery.' Her eyes did not flinch at all but held his, before she turned away with an apology to busy herself with the old man in the nearby bed who was coughing and wheezing uncontrollably.

Philip King turned on his heel and walked out of the door. For the first time in many years he felt that that he had been made to look foolish. By this chit of a girl too! Yet, as he was waylaid by the obsequious doctor he had arranged to meet in the Infirmary that morning, he was beginning to understand his son's fascination with her.

Much later that same day, Kate was walking towards the town square where she would meet the trap from Werrington. She too was wrapped in her thoughts when she heard her name being shouted from the doorway of the White Hart stables. It was the friendly voice of Isaac Penhale.

She stopped in her tracks and Isaac caught up with her. His eyes were twinkling with amusement.

'I hear you caused something of a stir over at Tregeare House a few weeks ago Miss Polglaze!' His face was flushed with the wine he'd consumed inside the coaching inn. 'Good for you, I say!'

'It's Kate, not Miss Polglaze! I thought we were past all the formalities, Isaac.' She smiled winningly at him. 'Well? What have you heard?'

'Oh I too called in to see Jasper, only a day or two after your visit!' He grinned at her like the proverbial madman. 'He's well and truly hooked you know. Even his spiteful sister can't put the poison in any more. He has convinced his doting mother that you, dear Kate, are the only woman for him!' He pretended to bow with a flourish, causing a couple of poor-looking women wrapped in dingy shawls to nudge each other before scuttling off across the square.

'So you were not impressed with Jasper's sister Elizabeth then Isaac?'
Kate smiled once more.

'She is the most puffed up... spoilt creature I know!' Isaac stopped, thinking back to their conversation at Tregeare. 'Yes she looks beautiful in an unreal way. But she was vicious about you, trying to persuade her mother that Jasper could do so much better for himself than get involved with what she called 'a working woman who looks like an unkempt gypsy from a hovel out on Bodmin Moor.'

He looked horrified when he realized what he had actually relayed to Kate. But she looked simply amused, as if she expected nothing more.

'All I can say is, I pity the poor chap who eventually marries Miss Elizabeth King!' Isaac looked at Kate's still serene face as he spoke.

'So it won't be you then, making her the next Lady Penhale!' Kate smiled at Isaac's fierce expression. There was a moment when they just looked at each other.

Then Isaac snorted loudly, 'Not for all the tin in the dear old county of Cornwall!' He laughed heartily then, and it was so infectious that eventually she could not resist joining in.

Chapter 40.

Spring had arrived with its fresh buds and primroses studding the hedgerows. The pastures were full of sheep grazing on the new grass. In the trees birds flitted to and fro, their beaks full of twigs in a frenzy of nest-building. Bird-song filled the air with the hope of new life.

At Badharlick new life was stirring within Mary Jane as the baby grew, hidden by layers of skirts and an apron. She looked prettier than ever, her skin glowing and her red-gold hair gleaming in the spring sunshine on the day William Treglown called in at Badharlick farmstead, insisting on speaking to her after so many months. She had kept close to her place of work lately, hiding in the room she shared up in the rafters, with Sarah as her only confidante. But that morning she happened to be out in the yard filling a bucket with cold, clean water at the pump, so there was no escaping seeing him.

He slid from his saddle with ease, the old injuries from the night of the robbery clearly mended. William's face lit up to see her once more. He had begun to think over the past months that something terrible had happened and that Mary Jane was near to death's door. Old Sarah had been evasive when questioned about her, refusing to look straight at him, but now he could see Mary Jane with his own eyes and he was relieved to see that she looked well. In fact, she looked positively blooming!

Mary Jane glimpsed William looping his mare's reins over the gate-post of the yard as she stood upright from her exertions of filling the bucket at the pump. There was nowhere for her to hide. He came towards her, his dear face smiling to see her after so long. He strode across the yard, took her hand and, after a quick glance up at the farmhouse windows, kissed her cheek. Oh so tenderly… It was unbearable to her.

She turned her head, murmuring 'Don't William.'

He, thinking it was because they might be being watched from her employer, relinquished her hands gently. 'What is it Mary Jane? I have been desperate to see you again after so many weeks. You have been ill, my dearest… but now I see that you are better once more!'

His kind eyes looked into her wide innocent ones with such concern. The past few months had been a nightmare, cooped up at home in Tregeare Green with his over-protective mother driving him to distraction. His mind had been full of Mary Jane, fearing that she was ill and dying. But now she stood in front of him, her hazel eyes seemingly full of emotion to see him again.

'I can't speak with you William,' she glanced nervously up at an open window.

'But we have an understanding between us Mary Jane. Don't we?' She said nothing, but her cheeks burned. 'You know that I am devoted to you. I have been ever since that day of the summer storm, down by the river, when we first met.'

'Tis all ruined now,' her voice was very quiet, barely audible.

'Well I know that the meadows are ruined, but that is because the railway company has started to lay out the plans for the building of the station…' his voice tailed off. 'It is all in the name of progress Mary Jane! Imagine how exciting it will be when we can both get on a train together at Egloskerry to travel to the sea-side! Or even to travel into Launceston by train on market days.'

She shook her head and sighed. 'Tis all different now William,' she forced herself to speak, mournfully, her eyes filling up.

He took a step back to look at her. 'The world is changing... and it will be for the better Mary Jane! I promise you.' He smiled at her and she weakened.

Suddenly the window above them opened wide and old Sarah's voice hissed out at them, 'Mary Jane! You must come in now maid. Missus is looking fer you and she's getting herself in a right old tizz!'

The girl picked up the bucket too quickly, slopping some of the fresh water, freeing herself. 'I must go now before there's trouble,' she said. 'She's terrible when she's proper angry.'

'I'll be back soon to see you again my dear Mary Jane,' William's voice was determined. 'Then I promise we'll talk somewhere without interruption.'

But other happenings intervened before the two met once more. In the village of Egloskerry the Post Office was abuzz with news. The women who liked to gossip had been forced to buy stamps or spices that they probably would not use for some time, so as to be in on the latest juicy snippets. It seemed that at Killicoff there had been uproar! One of the navvies had suddenly disappeared, without any say-so. But what was worse, he had gone off without paying for his lodgings and a valuable silver spoon, a family heirloom, was missing. It seemed that the Jenkin family had been taken for a ride.

'Well they've got their come-uppance if you don't mind me saying,' a thin-faced woman in dusty black nodded to herself with grim satisfaction.

'Oh no, I feel for poor Mrs. Jenkin,' a younger woman, a wife with a huge wicker basket on her arm, was more sympathetic. 'To be honest she didn't want they lodgers, not really. 'Twas her husband who was all for it, pushing and pushing, so that in the end she had to give in. Poor soul.'

A few voices murmured assent at this comment.

'I seed 'er at church last Sunday with her younger children, and she looked fair wiped out!' said another woman, wearing an ancient straw bonnet and a grubby apron.

'Tes all greed what does it.' A deep male voice in their midst caused consternation, revealing one of the more Hell-fire chapel-goers. He had been behind the shelf of glass jars with their indecipherable contents.

He appeared round the corner. 'The racket that went on in this village from they navvies like them lot up at Killicoff, out the Simcoe Arms the other evening, was nothing short of the work of the Devil himself! Tis the Demon Drink what does it! And in time we'll shut that there public house down.' He glared at the flustered females. 'You mark my words!' He slammed a couple of coins on the polished counter and, clutching his purchase tightly, he left the women open-mouthed. The Post mistress could have posted a letter in each and every one of them!

'Well I'm darned,' said the owner of the sticky bonnet. As if tedn't bad enough we must put up with all they navvies rampant in our midst, but we all get shouted at by that miserable toe-rag Thomas Treloar!'

The women subsided and the gossip about Killicoff switched to a young woman from Trebeath who had given birth to a baby with a strawberry mark on his head.

The Post Office bell tinkled and they stopped their talk, in case it was Thomas Treloar returned for his next rant about alcohol and wild drunken ways in their midst at Egloskerry. But it was the mother of young Sam Strike, the eavesdropper, who had hidden behind the wall of Church Cottage. The women perked up, noting that the normally placid Mrs. Strike looked fit to burst.

'Well neighbours, you won't believe what my boy Sam came out with this morning!' Her face glistened with her desperation to reveal all.

'Twas last Friday night at the Simcoe,' she stopped to think. 'Or was it the Thursday?'

'Go on Nancy! Dun't matter a jot what day it were!' said the woman with the wicker basket over her arm.

'Well twas like this...'

Before too long, Sam's account of the attack at Little Athill by navvies on that ansum young farmer William Treglown, from Tregeare Green, was out in the open.

The women gobbled up the tit-bits, chewed them over, and eventually scuttled off in their separate ways, leaving the Post Office a quiet little haven once more.

Along the road at Killicoff, Mary Jane's mother, wearing a hessian sacking apron, was on her knees scrubbing out the slate slabs in the dairy. The water was cold and fast becoming grey as she scrubbed. Her mind was full of recent events and the argument that had taken place when her husband had discovered that he had been swindled out of some money by one of his younger lodgers, who had quite simply vanished overnight on the previous Friday. The other navvies seemed to be as surprised as Jenkin had been at the sudden disappearance, shrugging their shoulders and shambling off to work as usual.

She had felt sad that it was the good-looking navvy who had left; he'd had a rather winning way with him, and he used to wink at her when her husband's back was turned. But she had not been prepared for the ranting and raving of her husband when the absence was discovered! The children had hidden away up in the top garden until their father had calmed down again, out of reach of a sudden stinging slap. The fact that the navvy had owed him lodge money, galled her husband beyond measure. He'd ranted that he 'would have strangled that cocky bugger if he'd just had the chance,' and to have stolen the Jenkin family's valuable silver spoon just rubbed salt in his wound.

Mary Jane's mother finished her scrubbing and stood up painfully, holding the small of her back. She ached all over these days. She stood out on the back step and sloshed the dirty water away with a loud sigh.

Meanwhile up in the vegetable patch her youngest child, Edith, played happily at mud pies. Her appealing face was smeared with dirt as she dug ferociously with a silver spoon.

The family's missing heirloom.

Chapter 41.

But there was more than a missing silver spoon to worry about in the Jenkin household. As the week wore on and whispers went around the village, three more navvies picked up their belongings from Killicoff one night and simply vanished, like the good-looking gypsy fellow the Friday before. Where they had gone not a soul knew, but Mary Jane's father flew into a rage like his long-suffering wife had never seen before. Four paying lodgers had slipped through his fingers... without a word of thanks. He stomped up and down in the kitchen like some kind of cooped-up wild animal, venting his spleen on any one, or anything, which got in his way. The cats cowered under the table and made their escape when the back door was opened. Even then a tabby had his scrawny backside kicked as he flew out past the pump! The children rushed off to school enthusiastically for once, preferring the schoolmistress's harsh words and the chance of the stick, rather than upset their own father who was obviously 'in a state' and best to be avoided. Only the youngest, Edith, remained at home and she trotted off to her mud pies, digging happily in a corner of the vegetable patch.

Down below in the river meadows in Egloskerry, the building of the railway station's foundations had begun. There was official talk that there would be the station building and signal box on the 'up' platform and a siding behind, which would serve the cattle pens. The local folk were at last beginning to realise that this great happening, the coming of the railway, was not going to go away. Some of the farmers began to scratch their heads and think how easy it would be to load up their cattle for transportation to the busy market in Launceston on Tuesdays.

There was even going to be something strange called 'a level crossing' at the 'down' end of the platform. Whatever that was, remained to be seen!

Then one day a cheerful bowler-hatted man from the railway company mingled amongst the menfolk, painting a colourful picture of how it would be in the future, with rabbits being transported from Camelford, minerals from Delabole and fish from far-off Padstow. There were major feats of engineering being carried out by gangers, a huge iron bridge was being built at some unknown place called Petherick Creek, plate-layers were grafting all hours to make this amazing thing happen! The future would be so exciting... Gradually railway fever was making itself felt amongst the villagers.

William Treglown was fascinated by all the railway talk. It was on everyone's lips in the busy cattle market in Launceston where he accompanied his father on Tuesdays. He no longer drove alone to market, for since the attack on him he had lost some of his confidence. But on a sunny day in May when the birds were singing loudly, he had been told the true story of the attack on him, by a young farmer friend, passed on down a line of people, originally from the mouth of Sam Strike himself. The tale may have changed a little in the re-telling, like the Christmas party game Chinese Whispers, but the gist of it was the truth. That the violent attack on him had been the work of four navvies, and they had quite simply scarpered into thin air!

The news had not surprised William one bit. His one regret was that he had not had the chance to land a punch on one, or all, of the gang who had stolen his money and left him with a fine old scar on his face which burned when he thought of those ruffians who had inflicted it on him. But for now he had more than that on his mind. He intended to visit Mary Jane and make absolutely clear the extent of his feelings towards her. She was a pretty, unblemished country girl with no daft airs and graces. What an asset she would be as a farmer's wife! His mother would just have to accept it and forget her 'mazed' notion of marrying him off to the neat, dark-haired schoolmistress in the tiny school at Tregeare Green. He had been captivated by a girl with a mass of red-gold hair, a real country girl. She was a child of nature, simple and uncomplicated.

He had not really managed to talk to Mary Jane properly on his last impromptu visit, as she was worried that they were being watched, no doubt. But now he was determined. He would contrive to meet her alone... and he felt sure in his heart that she felt the same about him.

Launceston was bustling that spring day, the butter market doing a roaring trade in its midst. In the narrow streets, cattle stood with their owners, awaiting buyers. There was muck and filth lying in the straw, all around. That was another thing, William thought to himself as he surveyed the scene. It was time someone came up with a plan to build a proper cattle market. After all, when the railway started bringing cattle in trucks from Egloskerry and outlying areas, business would boom surely. He imagined the drovers running down the winding path, Zig-Zag, to meet the trains before driving the stumbling beasts from the trains up to the town.

As he stood watching the busy scene with its mass of farmers in bowler hats and polished leather gaiters and farm labourers with some of the older men still wearing old-fashioned smocks, he noticed a smart gig pull up near the Little White Hart. He watched as Jasper King climbed down with some difficulty, helped by Ned, who had worked for the King family for donkeys' years it was said. There was something different about the once arrogant-looking Jasper, apart from the fact that he now walked with the aid of a silver-topped cane. So! The perfect son and heir of Tregeare House, was perfect no more, or so it seemed to William. Jasper King was still a handsome young man, but his face seemed to flinch with pain as he limped across the square, avoiding the packed crowd gathered around the gabbling auctioneer aloft on a cart amidst the pens.

Later that same day William saw Jasper once more, with Isaac Penhale from St. Clether. Folk said Penhale's father was slowly dying and their manor house and land was in a proper old mess; but Isaac's face showed none of his worries, laughing heartily with his friend Jasper, both men flushed with the effects of drink in some hostelry or other.

William's father had been looking at the horses for sale and doing some business. He was also looking very pleased with himself when he eventually lurched down the steps from the White Hart, having clinched a deal for a stunning chestnut mare earlier that day.

As he was leaving the market to return home to Tregeare Green with his father, William had a final glimpse of Jasper King talking to an exotic-looking young woman in a doorway. She had rather wild-looking black hair caught back with a scarlet ribbon, the only bright thing about her rather drab attire. Jasper's smiling face was illuminated in the dwindling rays of sunshine as he looked down at her. Yes, there was definitely something different about Jasper King from the Big House. It had seemingly taken a hunting accident and an unusual young woman to bring about the changes.

Chapter 42.

A pretty little wedding was solemnized in Tregeare Chapel towards the end of that summer. William Treglown, in best attire, scrubbed and handsome but with a scar burning brightly on his sun-weathered face, emerged from the shadowy chapel into the sunshine with his new bride. He stood in the chapel doorway as rigidly as a soldier on parade. His family clustered around the couple, his mother Joan smiling proudly at her beloved only son. His father's pained expression suggested that either his shirt collar was much too tight or he would have liked to be anywhere else but where he stood, preferably working with his horses. William's sister Eliza was bridesmaid, in a dress edged with old family lace. Their aged, wrinkled womanservant, Annie, who had mollycoddled William since he was a baby, wept copiously and noisily into a bleached white handkerchief, flapping it about like a flag of surrender.

William looked down at his bride, clinging to his arm possessively. He closed his own eyes momentarily and saw clear eyes with hazel lights and coppery-golden hair, illuminated in shafts of sunlight. When he opened them once more, he saw his bride's brown eyes darting to and fro like a little wren's, and her smooth dark hair in a tidy knot, adorned with a veil and a garland of summer flowers.

'I prayed that you would marry the village schoolmistress, William!' His bearded, Bible Christian grandfather nodded approvingly. 'Verity Hoskin's a trim little body, a clever little maid. Full of learning and Scripture and good works.'

In a dream-like state, William smiled weakly. Suddenly his knees went, and he staggered. What had he done? The words kept repeating themselves, over and over in his mind. He must try to regain his composure, to deal with the situation. It was, quite simply, his wedding day. But how do you smile and celebrate, when you know deep in your heart that you have just married the wrong woman?

The bride's family gathered outside the chapel, smiling and enjoying the joyous occasion. It seemed a small, happy gathering, but Verity's mother looked severe and calculating, her small black eyes gleaming behind her spectacles missing nothing. A terrible black crow came to William's mind. They always said that your bride would turn into her mother, down all the years. Down all the years... How could he face it all? William's mind was in a complete turmoil! The very thought of the marriage bed made him shudder. All of this was, of course, his very own fault. He had made his own bed, and now he must lie in it. How many times had he heard that old expression from Annie as she scrubbed out the pans in the dairy? Now he knew its bitter meaning at last.

And where was Mary Jane Jenkin in all this?

When William had returned from Launceston market with his father all those many weeks beforehand, he had been determined to see her as soon as it was possible. He had ridden to Badharlick the very next day, his mind full of the golden country girl he had often met down in the pastures tending the heifers the previous summer. She had invaded his thoughts from that first moment under the trees in dappled sunlight.

But when he had reined in his mare at the farm gates and dropped easily from the saddle, he had seen the anxious face of old Sarah peering out at him from an open window. Within minutes the ageing dairy-woman appeared breathlessly around the corner of the house, looking agitated as she wiped her work-worn hands in her soiled apron.

'If tis Mary Jane you'm after, sir, then you've wasted your journey.' She paused, puffing and blowing loudly as she leaned against the lichened wall. 'She bid me tell you sir, that she wishes you well, but she can't see you no more.'

William had half-expected something like this, from the tone of their last meeting. But he was determined to speak with Mary Jane herself, for he was sure of her true feelings for him. She had not been the same since her illness at Christmas, but on his last visit, albeit briefly, had he not seen her looking positively blooming in the spring sunshine?

He shook his head and laughed nervously at the old woman. 'No Sarah, I won't accept that. Not until I hear those words straight from Mary Jane's own mouth.' And what a beautiful mouth she had, red and ripe for his passionate kisses.

'You must go sir, afore mistress comes looking fer me.' Sarah rheumy old eyes were misting o'er to see that nice young man, William Treglown, struggling with his emotions. 'I'm sorry 'bout it sir, but that's how tis.' She turned her back on him and disappeared round the corner from whence she came, blowing her nose on her apron as she went.

He had stood like a statue for some minutes, staring towards the empty space where the old woman had been. Then with renewed intent, he strode after her, round the back of the house towards the shippen, the dairy and the stables.

Behind the scrubbed dairy, in the mowhay, he found her. Mary Jane was pegging out the freshly-washed cloths from the cheese-making on a make-shift washing line. She had not seen him watching from the shadow of the building.

It was a beautiful pastoral scene and William absorbed it greedily. An artist would have caught his breath to see it and wanted to capture it on canvas: the pretty country girl in her print dress, innocent and unaware of a watcher, her red-gold hair tumbling freely down over her shoulders, her sunburned arms reaching down to the basket at her feet as she stooped. Then she stretched up to the washing line to peg out the next cloth and William's life changed in that instant. The curve of her rounded belly was undeniable. There was a baby growing inside Mary Jane's belly! In his horrified vision, all her innocent child-like appeal, shattered in that very moment. She was not the same woman he thought he loved. She had deceived him with another man.

Hs face reflected his shock and horror. At that moment, something made her look towards the dairy, perhaps a movement or the hysterical bark of one of the farm dogs, and she saw William standing there, transfixed. Her hands relinquished the cheese-cloth and quickly covered her belly protectively, her expression a mix of tragedy and pleading for understanding.

William had not waited for an explanation. In his state of shock he had turned on his heels and left her there, a tragic figure illuminated in the warm May sunshine.

And now only a few months later, after a quick betrothal in the country custom, William Treglown had allowed himself to be rushed into marrying Verity Hocking the schoolmistress of Tregeare Green. He had not cared enough to fight it. He had been crushed by Mary Jane's obvious deception and events had carried him along, like a leaf spinning uncontrollably in the current of a river.

So William Treglown had become a respectable married man. He had not known the awful truth about the brutal rape of the young woman he really loved. It was some time later, when old Sarah was beginning to lose her mind that she had revealed Mary Jane's innocence to him in a confused, rambling story.

And Mary Jane Jenkin? She went into labour the day after William's marriage, giving birth hours later in the attic room at Badharlick to a dark-eyed baby boy, a tiny shrivelled child which did not survive more than a few hours. The baby was secretly buried in a quiet, dark corner, just outside the ivy-covered wall of Egloskerry churchyard, under the yew trees.

At Killicoff, only Mary Jane's mother had known about the baby, declaring it an act of nature. She was a simple woman, fearing the terrible anger of her husband, so she had schemed with old Sarah to keep the whole sad tale a secret from him.

Birth and death had been visited upon Mary Jane in quick succession. She would have to live with it for the rest of her life.

Chapter 43.

It was well over a year since after William Treglown's wedding. Mary Jane's baby had been born, died and was buried.

Now it was time for the arrival of the railway. It had finished off its slow snaking along the valley of the River Kensey, past the infamous Red Down cutting in the approaches to Egloskerry where the navvies had sweated and faced injury and even death.

On a day in October, Egloskerry station opened for all to see. A smart red-brick building with a signal box stood on the minty meadows where Mary Jane and William had met and fallen in love back in those humid summer days, amidst drowsy bees and the perfume of hay.

Crowds of people clustered excitedly around the station, awaiting the celebrations. The Iron Horse was about to gallop into their very midst and then on along the line to Tresmeer station in the hamlet named Splatt, before reaching Otterham Station high above sea level where it would be exposed and open to all the fury of Atlantic gales in the coming winter. Eventually the train would reach far-off Padstow, a fishing village on the North Cornish coast, connecting it with Waterloo Station in the busy capital city of London.

Among the crowd a few familiar faces could be seen from Badharlick. Mary Jane stood slightly apart from them, deep in her own thoughts, of those precious days in the past when she had walked through these sweet-scented meadows to meet William, before all the pasture land had been churned up and covered with red brick, wooden sleepers and metal tracks. It all seemed so very long ago.

Mary Jane was not bitter towards William, though she had good reason to be, for she had never even been given the opportunity to tell him the awful truth about the violent physical attack on her. She felt she had been more sinned against than sinning, and she had suffered greatly. She felt she had deserved William's pity at the very least. All those months later, helped by faithful old Sarah, she had given birth to a tiny baby boy who sickened after his first breath. He was now sleeping peacefully in his green bed under the quiet earth.

She sighed and tears filled her eyes. She brushed them away and forced herself to look along the crowded platform. Some of the dignitaries from Launceston, Egloskerry and the surrounding area were on a decorated raised area.

To the right of the Mayor, with his gold chain glinting in the early October sunshine, she saw a handsome looking couple. She recognized the unusual-looking woman with the tumbling mass of black hair. It was the woman who had driven past Badharlick on the road to Tregeare in a pony and trap and they had briefly locked eyes, a year or two before. Then she'd had an aura of unhappiness about her, dressed rather shabbily in her drab clothes. But now she was simply stunning, resplendent in a fashionable costume of bright autumn colours of orange and gold, her glossy ebony hair tamed under a wide-brimmed hat. The man next to her, leaning towards her on a silver-topped cane, seemed to be the reason she was smiling.

A man's deep voice next to Mary Jane answered the questions in her mind. 'That there Jasper King from the Tregeare estate's looking some bleddy pleased with hisself!'

'Wouldn't you be?' His pock-marked companion sounded bitter. 'That man King has every darned thing: a big house, the best horses an' cattle, and now 'tis said ee's about to wed that there ansum woman, wi' all that black hair. Tedn't right. Some men ha' the pick o' the crop in ivery way, it do seem to me.' He shook his head in disgust at the ways of the world.

The first man laughed, throwing his head back as he did so. 'Well I do wish the maid good luck if 'er is to live at Tregeare House wi' that there spoilt sister of 'is! Look at 'er... next to 'en.' He pointed. 'That maid like a china doll, wi' the whitey-yeller hair in them fancy blue clothes. 'Ave 'ee ever seed such a stuck-up creatur in yer life?'

'Tes true she allus looks like 'er as a bad smell under 'er nawse!' The pock-marked man sniffed loudly. There was a pause before he continued, 'They d'-say the young couple be goin' to live in some family town house in Southgate Street in Lanson fer a while, so 'er can still help at th' Infirmary. Old man King won't like that, nor will 'is missus!' He seemed to be pleased at this, grinning at last. 'They been saying in the Simcoe Arms that the woman, Miss Polglaze as she'm called, 'as been living wi' her sick aunt fer some while over t' Werrington. But I hear tell the aunt hev' recently died, so now there's nort to stop em getting wed.' He spat on the platform, to the disgust of two elderly ladies. 'Not even them high-an'-mighty Kings could stop their son Jasper getting the maid he wanted in the end!'

Mary Jane smiled involuntarily at the talk. So, even though her own heart ached, at least one young couple had seemingly found their way to happiness, against all the odds. Society had not kept them apart.

Jasper King and Kate Polglaze had kept faith with one another.

There was a sudden stirring among the crowd. The signal lever had been pulled inside the signal box to warn of the approaching train. The uniformed Guard had his whistle at the ready and waved a flag importantly. People craned their necks, trying to get a glimpse along the humming track to the bend where the rails disappeared from view. A plume of greyish-black smoke could be seen in the distance, chuffing into the sky above the sloping curves of the pastureland.

The train could be seen coming around the bend, still some way off. The crowd swayed excitedly and many voices cheered loudly. Railway mania had come, at last, to North Cornwall! A few hats were thrown in the air and clumsily caught, children waved their own home-made flags on sticks and the Mayor of Launceston stood to attention and smoothed his gold chain on his robes. Next to him was the Squire of Egloskerry, and the Vicar, nervously standing slightly behind the others, his cassock sponged and brushed to look more presentable for the occasion. These important figures in the local community were now prepared to meet the amazing new arrival: a steam train puffing its way through the Cornish countryside from London, the greatest city of England where noble men and women lived out their lives. Where the men had never ploughed a furrow and where the women had never even milked a cow! Their country landscape would be connected with so-called 'Civilisation' at long last.

Bells clanged loudly and the platform was a hive of activity. The metal wheels gleamed in the sunlight and they clanked heavily as the train, draped in garlands, drew ever closer. Steam was hissing from its engine, sounding like a venomous snake while the polished carriages smoothly, almost soundlessly, were winding on behind.

Mary Jane remembered William's comforting words to her about the building of a railway station and the wonderful train rides they would share in the dim and distant future. All that was gone, faded into one brief summer of love and simmering passion, when the pasture land was unspoilt.

And so was she.

As if on cue, a sudden push from the crowd revealed William Treglown, craning his neck to get a clearer view, his face lit up at the sight of the train with its gleaming carriages. Next to him, clinging on to his arm like lichen to the branch of a tree, was a small, neatly-dressed dark-haired woman. Verity Treglown, his wife of one year.

Mary Jane recoiled, but not before his restless excited eyes had seen her. That moment sent a thrill through them both, quickly fading to momentary despair, and then sudden awareness of the present time. The girl with the glorious red-gold hair shrank back into the crowd, the people closing around her, while the man felt the possessive tugging at his arm and looked down at the lawful wedded wife at his side. He felt an indescribable pain, in his heart.

'He had made his bed... now he must lie in it.'

The speeches began, cheers and applause rang out. A small brass band started up on the platform, all was celebration and delight. The doubts and arguments over land were well and truly over, this great happening would be the making of North Cornwall! The railway had arrived at Egloskerry at long last, before continuing its winding way to the open sea.

The navvies and sawyers, tough work-hardened men, had finished their incredibly hard graft and moved on, scattering like beads of mercury across the country. Their former lodgings bore no sign that they were ever there, the takings in the public houses were depleted. The Simcoe Arms was peaceful once more, left to the old men and their stories. The village school was suddenly emptier and young girls and women mourned their secret lost lovers.

In a quiet corner under a yew tree in unconsecrated ground yet close by the churchyard wall, a tiny baby as dark as a gypsy, lay in everlasting sleep never having known his navvy father.

The wind whispered over the rough grass and soon it was gone.

Epilogue

The following summer a terrible railway accident happened at Egloskerry on the level crossing, which had already been causing some problems. It was June, hot old weather, the air stagnant and many of the pastures brown. A pair of dusty-looking horses, harnessed to a heavy wagon plodded along, exhausted in the heat. They were being driven across the level crossing at Egloskerry Station. The driver of the wagon, old Dawe, was known to be as deaf as a post. He did not hear the approach of a train, saw too late the gleaming wheels and cranks. Both of the terrified horses were caught by the engine and killed outright. It was a scene of carnage. Old Dawe the wagon-driver was also badly injured, with what was described as 'a severe scalp wound' but miraculously he somehow survived. The infamous level crossing, the only one on the line between Halwill Junction and Wadebridge, had done its worst. It was the talk of North Cornwall and the local newspapers had a field day.

After that tragedy, in the village of Egloskerry, life went on pretty much as it had before the arrival of the navvies. Babies were born, weddings took place in the church and chapel, old men tottered out of the Simcoe Arms and never came back. Funerals were hugely attended, with men in solemn black and women in black feathered hats.

But the cattle were driven down to the holding pens at the station, loaded into railway trucks and taken in to the market at Launceston every Tuesday. That had certainly made life much easier, the farmers agreed.

And what of Mary Jane Jenkin?

She never did get her dream visits to the seaside on the train. She turned to hard work on the farm, and her family, but she still harboured close to her heart those idyllic months spent with William down in the summer meadows.

'Those were the days,' she thought. 'The days before the railway puffed its way through minty meadows, towards the sea.'

But there were those who made much of their journeys on the train: Thomas Hardy on his way to St. Juliot vicarage where he would meet Emma Gifford, the woman he would fall in love with and marry; John Betjeman, the poet, on his well-recorded journeys to Padstow and then across the estuary to Trebetherick.

If Mary Jane could have lived until 1966, she would have seen the end of the railway line in North Cornwall; the end of what had become known as The Withered Arm. The last train left the station at Launceston in October that year, to make its final farewell to Egloskerry. It was packed with people, many with tears in their eyes, saying their own emotional goodbyes.

The ghosts of the navvies watched silently as the train passed them by.

No more would trains full of holiday-makers be heading to the Cornish coast from London. No more would excited city children wave from carriage windows as the engine puffed out of Launceston, on their way to sandy beaches and bucket-and-spade heaven. No more would the children of Launceston watch and wave in return, from the railway banks of Tredydan Road and Treloar Terrace.

There were no more trucks of cattle to be transported in to the busy market at Launceston every Tuesday, the drovers running down the steep winding path called Zig-Zag to unload them at the station.

The railway stations were deserted and empty. Rust-coloured engines lay in their own sad grave-yards. Tangled weeds and Rose Bay Willow herb grew profusely along the line. Soon the rusting rails and sleepers had disappeared too.

It was as if the railway had never been.

Author's Note

This novel is a mix of historical fact and fiction, set in the rural area of North Cornwall in the late 1800's, a time of new ideas and great change. It centres on the ancient market town of Launceston and the nearby parish of Egloskerry, including the hamlets of Tregeare and Badharlick. The novel is set at the turbulent time of the construction of the railway line with the arrival of its fearsome navvies in a peaceful country area of villages and isolated farms. Eventually Egloskerry parish would be connected with the fishing village of Padstow on the North coast, and busy Waterloo Station in London, a world away!

Part of the fascination for me was finding out that a group of railway navvies came to live in Killicoff in Egloskerry, where my mother was born and lived with her large family of brothers and sisters.

The characters in my novel are mostly fictional. But there are some characters mentioned who were real people:

- Philip Gidley King, who sailed with the first fleet of convicts to Botany Bay and became the third Governor of New South Wales
- Reverend Simcoe, who bought Penheale Manor in 1830 and later gifted land for the building of the railway station at Egloskerry
- Isambard Kingdom Brunel, designer and civil engineer of the famous Royal Albert Bridge over the Tamar at Saltash
- The Duke of Northumberland, whose seat was Werrington Park
- The Duke of Bedford, one of many who subscribed generously to the building of the railway

Some characters are also 'a mix' of fact and fiction. Philip King in the novel lives at stunning Tregeare House, being a descendant of the illustrious Philip Gidley King. Others are purely fictional, like Mary Jane Jenkin of Killicoff, a true child of nature.

I am indebted to the books I have consulted while creating this work of fiction. Among them are:
'Thomas Brassey Railway Builder' by Charles Walker,
'North Cornwall Navvies' by George Benbow,
'Yesterday's Town: Launceston' by Arthur Bate Venning and Arthur Wills,
'On the Slow Train' by Michael Williams,
'Philip Gidley King' by Carol Bunbury
'In Sundry places' the story of the Cornish estate of Tregeare, by C.W.R.Winter

Thank you to David Perry for his beautiful cover photograph. Thanks also to Roger Pyke of the 'Launceston Then' web-site, which has fascinating stories of people and days gone by in North Cornwall and which has captivated us all...

Finally thank you to my patient husband Jim, who probably feels that he has been on this railway journey with me for the last couple of years.

Jane Nancarrow

Jane Nancarrow was born in her grandparents' house at St. Stephen's, Launceston, Cornwall. She attended the old National School where she was taught by the poet Charles Causley, whose poetry and writing captured her imagination. She was a student of Launceston College and trained as a secondary teacher in Derby, where she played the role of Regan, Duchess of Cornwall in 'King Lear'. She returned to Cornwall and taught English at Bodmin College for thirty years, followed by some ten years of supply teaching. She has written numerous short stories and performed with local theatre companies in a variety of productions over the years, starting in the early days with Mary Yellan in 'Jamaica Inn' and most recently with the 'challenging' role of Celia in 'Calendar Girls'. She also appeared with Edward Woodward in his final film, 'A Congregation of Ghosts' filmed at Warleggan and on Bodmin Moor.

Jane Nancarrow's short stories have been published in Scryfa and in 2008 she won the Gorsedd prize for a short story set in Cornwall. Her debut novel 'Stones and Shadows' was published in 2010 and won praise from the prolific novelist E V Thompson who described it as 'evocative and intriguing.'

Her second novel 'Echoes at Endsleigh' was published in 2013, partly based on the diaries of her grandmother Bessie, once a housemaid at Endsleigh House for the Duke of Bedford in the beautiful Tamar Valley.

'Through Minty Meadows' is Jane Nancarrow's third novel.